Praise for the

The Gre

One of the big loves I had for this book, among other things, was it is so full of rich dialog. I am a sucker for running dialog that fills a story, it gets me to relate to the characters even more because you just have their voices and direct interaction running in your mind's eye throughout the story and Ms. Hill does this brilliantly. There isn't much angst in regard to the MCs, just a heartwarming holiday story, which can be read anytime of the year, of Nic just trying to make it through the holiday (again no spoilers, but me wiping away a few tears) and Abby slowly falling for Nic.

-Carol C., *NetGalley*

The Great Charade really is a heartwarming, romantic holiday book that I'm really glad I was able to read this season. If you're looking for a great novel to read this holiday, this may be the one you are looking for.

-Betty H., *NetGalley*

Red Tide at Heron Bay

One of the best things I love about Ms. Hill's writing is she takes the time to describe the environment and surroundings within the story, not so much as to stall the storyline but more to enhance the feeling of really being there with the characters... Ms. Hill does a wonderful job of blending mystery with a love story (reminds me of *Devil's Rock* and *Hell's Highway*) and she did it justice again in this book.

-Carol C., *NetGalley*

Love the Hawaiian shirts and the person wearing them. This romantic intrigue had my attention from the beginning. Detective Harley Shepherd, upbeat yet sad as she deals with the loss of someone close to her. Lauren Voss, resort manager, shying away from relationships as she continues to deal with a relationship that went off the rails. Both women "ran" to Heron Bay to heal. Little did they know that tragedy would be waiting for them right around the corner. I enjoyed the flirting and teasing. Some of the comments had me chuckling and laughing out loud.

-Kennedy O., NetGalley

The Stars at Night

The Stars at Night is a beautiful mountain romance that will transport you to a paradise. It's a story of self-discovery, family, and rural living. This romance was a budding romance that snuck-up and on two unsuspecting women who found themselves falling in love under the stars and while gazing at birds. It's a feel-good slow-burn romance that will make your heart melt.

-Les Rêveur

Hill is such a strong writer. She's able to move the plot along through the characters' dialogue and actions like a true boss. It's a masterclass in showing, not telling. The story unfolds at a languid pace which mirrors life in a small, mountain town, and her descriptions of the environment bring the world of the book alive.

-The Lesbian Review

Gillette Park

This book was just what I was hoping for and wickedly entertaining. The premise of this book is really well done. Parts are hard to read of course. This book is about a serial killer who targets mostly young teenagers. The book isn't very graphic, but it still breaks your heart in places. But there is also a sweet romance that helps to give the book a sense of hope. Mix that with some strong women, the creepiness of the paranormal factors, and the book balances out really well. There is a lot of potential with these characters and I'd love to see their stories continue. If you are a Hill fan, grab this.

-Lex Kent's Reviews, *goodreads*

Hill is a master writer, and this one is done in a way that I think will appeal to many readers. Don't just discount this one because it has a paranormal theme to it! I think that the majority of readers who love mystery novels with a romantic side twist will love this story.

-Bethany K., *goodreads*

It was suspenseful and so well written that it was anyone's guess what would happen next! The characters—all of them, as you'll learn, were perfectly written.

-Gayle T., *NetGalley*

Gerri Hill has written another action-packed thriller. The writing is excellent and the characters engaging. Wow!

-Jenna F., *NetGalley*

…is a phenomenal book! I wish I could give this more than five stars. Yes, there is a paranormal element, and a love story, and conflict, and danger. And it's all worth it. Thank you, Gerri Hill, for writing a brilliant masterpiece!

-Carolyn M., NetGalley

After the Summer Rain

…is a heartwarming, slow-burn romance that features two awesome women who are learning what it really means to live and love fully. They're also learning to let go of their turbulent pasts so that it doesn't ruin their future happiness. Gerri Hill has never failed to give me endearing characters who are struggling with heartbreaking issues, and beautiful descriptions of the landscapes that surround them.

-*The Lesbian Review*

Gerri Hill is simply one of the best romance writers in the genre. This is an archetypal Hill, slightly unusual characters in a slightly unusual setting. The slow-burn romance, however, is a classic, trying not to fall in love, but unable to fight the pull.

-*Lesbian Reading Room*

After the Summer Rain is a wonderfully heartfelt romance that avoids all the angsty drama-filled tropes you often find in romances.

-*C-Spot Reviews*

Moonlight Avenue

Moonlight Avenue by Gerri Hill is a riveting, literary tapestry of mystery, suspense, thriller and romance. It is also a story about forgiveness, moving on with your life and opening your heart to love despite how daunting it may seem at first.

-*The Lesbian Review*

...is an excellent mystery novel, sheer class. Gerri Hill's writing is flawless, her story compelling and much more than a notch above others writing in this genre.

-*Kitty Kat's Book Review Blog*

The Locket

This became a real page-turner as the tension racked up. I couldn't put it down. Hill has a knack for combining strong characters, vulnerable and complex, with a situation that allows them to grow, while keeping us on our toes as the mystery unfolds. Definitely one of my favorite Gerri Hill thrillers, highly recommended.

-*Lesbian Reading Room*

The Neighbor

It's funny...Normally in the books I read I get why the characters would fall in love. Now on paper (excuse the pun), Cassidy and Laura should not work...but let me tell you, that's the reason they do. I actually loved this book so hard. ...Yes it's a slow burn but so beautifully written and worth the wait in every way.

-Les Rêveur

This is classic Gerri Hill at her very best, top of the pile of so many excellent books she has written, I genuinely loved this story and these two women. The growing friendship and hidden attraction between them is skillfully written and totally engaging...This was a joy to read.

-Lesbian Reading Room

I have always found Hill's writing to be intriguing and stimulating. Whether she's writing a mystery or a sweet romance, she allows the reader to discover something about themselves along with her characters. This story has all the fun antics you would expect for a quality, low-stress, romantic comedy. Hill is wonderful in giving us characters that are intriguing and delightful that you never want to put the book down until the end.

-The Lesbian Review

TIMBER FALLS

Other Bella Books by Gerri Hill

After the Summer Rain
Angel Fire
Artist's Dream
At Seventeen
Behind the Pine Curtain
Chasing a Brighter Blue
The Cottage
Coyote Sky
Dawn of Change
Devil's Rock
GillettePark
The Great Charade
Gulf Breeze
Hell's Highway
Hunter's Way
In the Name of the Father
Keepers of the Cave
The Killing Room
The Locket
Love Waits
The Midnight Moon
Moonlight Avenue
The Neighbor
No Strings
One Summer Night
Paradox Valley
Partners
Pelican's Landing
The Rainbow Cedar
Red Tide at Heron Bay
The Roundabout
Sawmill Springs
The Scorpion
The Secret Pond
Sierra City
Snow Falls
The Stars at Night
Storms
The Target
Weeping Walls

About the Author

Gerri Hill has over forty-one published works, including the 2021 GCLS winner for *Gillette Park*, the 2020 GCLS winner *After the Summer Rain*, the 2017 GCLS winner *Paradox Valley*, 2014 GCLS winner *The Midnight Moon*, 2011, 2012 and 2013 winners *Devil's Rock*, *Hell's Highway* and *Snow Falls*, and the 2009 GCLS winner *Partners*, the last book in the popular Hunter Series, as well as the 2013 Lambda finalist *At Seventeen*. Gerri lives in south-central Texas, only a few hours from the Gulf Coast, a place that has inspired many of her books. With her partner, Diane, they share their life with two Australian shepherds—Rylee and Mason—and a couple of furry felines. For more, visit her website at gerrihill.com.

Bella Books, Inc.
P.O. Box 10543
Tallahassee, FL 32302

Printed in the United States of America on acid-free paper.

First Edition - 2022

Editor: Medora MacDougall
Cover Designer: Kayla Mancuso

ISBN: 978-1-64247-392-6

TIMBER FALLS

GERRI HILL

BELLA
BOOKS
2022

CHAPTER ONE

"So, listen to this," Haley said as she scrolled through her phone. "They found a guy stabbed fifty-four times and pretty much hacked to bits. In a motel room in Albuquerque. Can you imagine? A housekeeper comes in and finds that mess?"

"That's why I'm still single. You can't trust women."

"Why would you assume a woman did it? They suspect it was a drug deal gone bad. The motel is apparently a known meeting place for that sort of thing. Besides, I don't think a woman would have the stomach for that kind of killing."

Mike shook his head. "Another reason why I got out of the city. People are freaking crazy. I like it just fine up here where my only concern is an occasional fender bender and breaking up drunken fights when the river rats get into it."

The "up here" was Timber Falls, a little mountain village that stayed alive only because of the tourists who gathered there each summer. River rats, mostly. And the campers and RVers who wanted to get off the beaten path. Timber Falls wasn't at all accessible, really. Only one road came into town, dead-ending at Main Street before turning into a bumpy forest road that climbed into the mountains. The town was buffered by a high mountain pass on one side—at twelve thousand feet—and a winding road on the other that followed the river and slashed through town. That road—the only road—would take you down to Amber Springs, the closest town with amenities within two hours' drive in any direction.

Timber Falls had barely a hundred full-time residents, yet during the summer months when the river was swollen, several thousand tourists crowded into town. The one motel as well as the lodge stayed booked into September. The RV parks were packed as were the forest campgrounds in the area. The Timber River flowed through town in cascades of rapids with several nice chutes that could be challenging. Two outfitters ran the river, offering up raft trips all summer long for those who wanted to test their skills on the Class V rapids.

She poured him another cup of coffee. "How long have you been here, Mike? Ten years?"

"Yep. It'll be ten in July. And you're what? Seven?"

"This will be my seventh summer, yes. I bought the place in the fall, right after the tourists left. Moved here in January, remember?"

Mike Goodson—Chief Goodson—was her best customer and closest friend in town. When she'd bought the saloon, now officially named the Timber Falls Bar and Grill, he'd been the first one to come by and welcome her to town. Not that she hadn't already been familiar with it. She'd spent every summer of her college years working on the river. She and Gail.

The front door opened and the bell jingled, signaling a customer. She glanced at the wall clock, not much past six thirty. She opened at six each morning and Mike usually came by then for coffee and sometimes breakfast. It gave them time to visit, which, during tourist season, was about the only free time either of them had. Especially now. Curtis and Molly had left her unexpectedly two weeks ago, heading back to New Mexico to tend to Molly's ailing mother. That left her alone to work the breakfast crowd—serving as waitress and cook both. She now realized how much she had come to rely on them.

"Good morning," she called to the young couple who entered. "Pick any table you want. I'll bring coffee."

She glanced at Mike. "Time to start my day."

"I thought you were going to switch up the hours on one of your seasonal workers."

"I am. CeCe is going to switch from nights in exchange for being off this whole week. She's got friends in town. So, five more days. I can do it. Sylvia comes in at ten and Rhonda at noon."

She grabbed the coffeepot and plastered a smile on her face. The couple had chosen a table near the corner window that looked out at both the road in front and the river to the side. It was too early for the rafts to run, but it was still a beautiful sight. Each table had place settings and coffee cups turned upside down—Molly's doing. It saved them having to juggle cups and coffeepot at once.

The couple, a young man and woman in their late twenties, she guessed, had already turned the cups over. She filled them both. The woman reached for two sugar packets from the basket on the table and the man yawned and grabbed a creamer.

"Are you running the river today?" she asked, reminding herself to make pleasant conversation with the customers, something else Molly had taught her. God, she missed them.

"Yes. Our tour starts at nine. We're doing the long one."

"Oh, that's fun. Dead Man Falls, just outside of town, will have you screaming."

"That's what we hear. We put in yesterday just past that, so we missed it," the woman said. "It was still fun."

"Well, I hope you have a good time today. Do you need a moment to look over the menu or would you like to order?"

"Oh, give us a little while. I just want to drink my coffee and wake up," the woman said. "We're camping. Unfortunately, most of our neighbors are college kids. They didn't quiet down until about two this morning."

"Tell the camp hosts. They'll talk to them. That's what they're there for."

"Yes, I think we will. Thanks."

She topped off Mike's cup before putting the coffeepot back on the warmer. "What are you going to have this morning? A taco or a plate?"

"Better make it a taco. Chorizo and egg. I'll take it with me."

"Why in a hurry?"

"I haven't been to my house in weeks. I'm doing laundry this morning before making my rounds."

"Since Curtis and Molly left, I haven't been to my house either."

"You staying in the apartment upstairs?"

"Through this week. Once CeCe changes shifts, she can handle it until about seven. That's when the breakfast crowd starts rolling in and that's when I'll roll in too."

She went into the kitchen to start his breakfast when his cell rang. She only absently listened to him talk as she cracked two eggs onto the greased griddle. Just as she put the chorizo on, Mike stuck his head inside the kitchen.

"Got to run. No time for breakfast."

She glanced at him, seeing the ashen look on his face. "What's wrong?"

"Hell, they…they found a guy dead."

She paused, spatula in hand. "Dead? They who?"

"That was David, one of the campground hosts. Says it's a goddamn bloody mess out there."

"Oh my god. A bear attack?"

"Don't know." He pointed at the griddle. "Sorry about that."

"No problem. I'll have it myself." When he turned to leave, she called after him. "Let me know what's going on."

"I will."

Even if her choices for friends wasn't limited, Mike was still the best. They were probably the youngest two in town—him at forty and she at thirty-three. Youngest of the locals, that is. During tourist season, everyone hired seasonal help, including her. Mostly college students wanting to earn enough money to allow them to stay up here all summer. She was lucky in that regard. The old saloon had four rooms upstairs—a brothel at one time, she'd been told—in addition to the small apartment. Curtis and Molly had lived in the apartment—where she'd been staying this week—but she offered free housing and restaurant meals in exchange for work. Well, not totally an even exchange. She did pay a small salary in addition to the room and board. All four rooms had two twin beds, so she hired eight seasonal workers each summer. Fortunately, they usually returned for two, sometimes three years. Hers was one of the few places in town that could offer housing in addition to a salary.

She mindlessly made the taco, wrapping it up in foil and placing it under the warmer. She would have it later when there was a lull. She looked around the kitchen with a sigh. Hard to believe she'd been here that long—her seventh summer. Even harder to believe that Gail had been gone for eight. Eight years come June.

Sometimes it seemed like only yesterday.

And sometimes a lifetime ago.

CHAPTER TWO

To say Timber Falls was abuzz was an understatement. Every person who came in had a different story, it seemed, and Haley had lost count of all the purported causes of death.

"Damn near had his head cut off, I heard." That from Butter Bill, the large, round man who always claimed the last barstool on the far end.

Another local, Scott Carlton, said he heard there was a trail of blood heading to the river. "Had to have been a bear."

"Ain't no black bear going to attack a sleeping man for no good reason. I heard there wasn't even any food in his tent. Wasn't no bear," claimed Charlie Wadsworth, an old, grizzled widower who had been living in Timber Falls since he was a boy.

"Haley? Not a word from Mike yet?"

She shook her head as she filled a mug with draft beer. "I called him. All he said was it was a hell of a mess. I'm sure he'll be by later, and we can all catch up."

"Bound to have scared those young river rats," Charlie said with a gravelly chuckle.

"Rafts been running all day, same as usual," Bill said. "I called Sam up myself. He said he didn't have a single cancellation."

"Don't know why folks would cancel a river run because of a bear attack," Scott said as he sipped from his beer.

"I told you, it wasn't no bear," Charlie insisted.

Haley left them with a smile, leaving them to argue among themselves. Despite Charlie's assertion, she was leaning toward bear attack too. The multitude of sheriff's cars coming and going all day begged to differ, however. The bell dinged, signaling an order was ready and she turned to the serving window, seeing Sylvia hunched over the griddle, flipping burgers. She was seventy-eight years old and only one of two locals who worked for her. Rhonda worked noon to six during the summer, when the seasonal employees were there. In winter, she shifted to nights, coming in at five and staying until closing. The tourists and river rats started dwindling in August, when fall classes started up again and the river had lost its ferocious flow. By late September, when the aspens had turned golden, the tourists left altogether. The shops closed up then, including the one other restaurant in town besides her, and Flip's Diner. Flip served breakfast—mostly pancakes—and lunch only and closed up at two each day in the winter, leaving her as the only choice for dinner and drinks once the tourists were gone. A little over a hundred souls called Timber Falls home during the winter months and a lot of them hung out at the saloon, grabbing dinner and drinks and catching up on gossip.

It was a routine she was well versed in now and she quite enjoyed the break. Of course, that was when Curtis and Molly had been there. They'd stumbled into her life that first year when she'd been struggling. Curtis had simply taken over the kitchen, and she'd let him. She wondered if she'd even been able to make a go of things without them.

She leaned against the open kitchen door, looking down the bar, then out over the dining room. It was going on five o'clock. The river runs were all but over for the day. She'd seen the vans coming back, the roofs holding two, sometimes three rafts. The vans shuttled the rafters back up to Timber Falls River Outfitters or just past that to Sam's place—Sam's River Runners. By six the saloon would be crowded and noisy, the country music she could still hear now would be relegated to the background as conversations and laughter dominated.

Yes, this was all familiar and routine to her now. She tried to recall her previous life, but it was blurry. Like the corporate job she'd had in downtown Denver, stuck in a tiny cubicle on the fifth floor—she barely remembered it. Her title had been Investment Research Analyst, but she'd done little more than run reports all day long, giving the information to someone else to decipher. The salary was decent, but she'd been bored out of her mind.

After Gail's accident, she'd simply quit one day, knowing she couldn't go through the motions any longer. She came out here to Timber Falls, a place she and Gail had visited each summer during college. She'd gone into the Timber Falls Saloon one night to drown her sorrows. Eddie and Charlotte—who had owned the bar for sixteen years—told her they were putting it up for sale. They had visions of warmer weather, buying a boat, and fishing the Florida Keys. She had gone to bed that night dreaming of buying the place.

Her grandmother had told her she was setting herself up for failure at a young age—she'd been twenty-six at the time—but had loaned her the money nonetheless. She changed the name and pretty much everything else about the one-time bar. The most drastic change was opening for breakfast and lunch. The old saloon had opened at three and closed at midnight, serving only alcohol and tasteless bar food—burgers and wings that had come precooked and frozen.

She'd had no clue what she was doing and, thankfully, Curtis and Molly had walked into her life. Indeed, if they hadn't, she imagined her grandmother's words would have rung true. But it wasn't a failure. Quite the opposite. Her profit margin on food wasn't huge, but she made a killing on alcohol sales. As she'd known back in college, river rats loved to drink.

The bell jingled on the front door, and she turned toward it, seeing Mike come shuffling in. She went to the bar, having his mug filled before he could even sit down. Charlie, Scott, and Butter Bill were on him in a flash, demanding answers. Mike held his hand up, silencing them.

"Can I at least have a swallow of beer first?"

"It was a bear, wasn't it?" Scott asked.

"Without a doubt, no."

"Told you it wasn't a bear," Charlie interjected.

Mike took a big swallow of beer, then put his mug down with a sigh. "Damn long day."

"Yeah, yeah. But what's going on?" Bill asked as he scooted his barstool closer.

"Let's just say I'm glad the sheriff's department has jurisdiction and not me."

"Shit. Was it a murder?"

He nodded. "As you all know, I worked in LA back in the day, and I've never seen anything like this. That poor guy was stabbed fifty or more times. He had fingers cut off, his ears cut off." Mike shuddered. "His penis was—"

"Whoa. *No!*"

"Yeah, it was."

"Who was he?" Haley asked.

"Name was Hayden Anderson, age twenty. He was here with four buddies."

"So what happened?" Scott asked.

"Don't know. No one heard a thing. Some guy going down to the river this morning saw all the blood outside the tent." He paused. "Blood and, well, several fingers."

"Jesus Christ," Bill murmured. "So this kid was hacked up and you have no suspects?"

Mike glared at him. "I'm not in charge of this. Like I said, the sheriff's department has jurisdiction."

"Lucky for you."

"Yeah, lucky for me, considering I'm a one-man show here."
He took another swallow of beer. "From what I hear, the FBI
is going to be involved. This matches another killing from last
week."

Haley's eyes widened. "Oh my god! What I was reading you
this morning about the guy in Albuquerque? Is that it?"

He nodded. "They believe so. Thought it was drug-related
at first. Turns out that guy was camping too. A backpacker. Solo
hiker. Just came off the trail and grabbed a motel for the night."

"Damn bad luck there," Butter Bill said.

"So they think some guy is on a killing spree and he's
targeting campers? Damn. What are the chances he picked our
little town?" Scott asked.

"Would have rather it been a bear," Charlie muttered.

"Heard there was a trail of blood to the river," Scott said.
"That true?"

"Sure was. It was a damn bloody mess, I tell you. We figure
the killer did his thing, then went to the river to clean up."

"So maybe it's another camper," Haley suggested.

"It's a large campground, lots of people there," Mike said.
"We interviewed most of them. Those that we got to before the
river runs started anyway. That particular campground, most all
of them are college students. By all accounts, Hayden Anderson
was a fun-loving guy, well-liked. No one knew of any fights or
disagreements. No one heard a thing last night. Nothing."

Haley leaned on the bar. "Is this something we should be
concerned about? I mean, you think we've got a killer in town?"

"Hell, I don't know. Is it a serial killer traveling the state,
hacking up hikers? Are there more that haven't been found yet?"

"Or more to come," Bill said quietly in an ominous tone.

Haley nodded. "I guess we should be thankful the FBI will
have a presence here." She looked at Mike. "They will, right?
Have a presence? Or will they leave like the sheriff's deputies
do?"

"Should have someone in town tomorrow. I imagine
someone from the sheriff's department will make the trip up
too. As far as I know, it's still their gig. The FBI is coming on
board because of the other killing."

"The sheriff's department needs an office here, plain and simple," Charlie said. "Forty miles up the mountain is too damn far away. If we have an emergency, it takes them over an hour to get up here."

"Now, Charlie, you know damn well they're not going to put an office up here. We barely have a hundred people who live here full time."

"I'm just sayin'."

"Yeah, well, save your breath."

"Need two draft beers," Rhonda called. "Coors Light."

Haley nodded, then went to fill the order. Was she worried? Maybe if she was at home by herself. But living here in the apartment upstairs, there were eight others just down the hall. She felt safe here. There was safety in numbers, she thought. That old saying rang true.

Didn't it?

CHAPTER THREE

Carter drove slowly through town, wondering if this was all there was to it. Not a town. A little mountain village was more like it. She spotted the faded POLICE sign hanging on a wall of a building that was crammed between two shops selling T-shirts and gifts. The shop doors were propped open, and T-shirts fluttered from the breeze. She pulled to a stop, looking around a bit before getting out. Murdock had told her to look up Mike Goodson. He would take her to the crime scene. The sheriff's department was due there by noon. She glanced at the black watch on her wrist. It was 9:36. To be fair, she'd told them noon, thinking she'd be too tired after her late flight to Durango to make an early morning of it. Instead, she'd been up before daybreak and had been on the road in time to catch the sunrise.

She paused on the sidewalk, watching as tourists mingled in front of shop windows. She guessed there were eight or ten different stores. All appeared to cater to tourists. At the far end, she saw a sign for GROCERY and another for POST OFFICE.

She went to the door of the police station and opened it. Sitting at a desk was an older woman with short, no-nonsense gray hair. She looked up, her eyes scanning her above the rim of her glasses.

"May I help you?"

"I'm looking for Chief Goodson."

"Oh, I'm sorry. He's out."

Carter stared at her blankly. "I think he's expecting me." She pulled out her credentials, still not used to them. "Special Agent Carter, ma'am. FBI."

The woman looked her over head to toe, taking in her comfortable faded jeans, the gun and holster at her hip, the hiking boots that were newly scuffed, and the black T-shirt. Carter smiled at her. "Yes, I really am FBI."

The woman put her glasses on more firmly as she peered at her picture. "Well, I've only seen FBI agents on TV before. The women are usually dressed…well, different."

Carter folded the leather case and shoved it into the back pocket of her jeans. "So? The chief?"

"I guess I could call him."

"That would be great. Thanks."

She turned away, going to stand at the window, looking out to give the woman some privacy. She had no idea what to expect from this small-town police department. She supposed it didn't much matter. The sheriff's department was to be her point of contact. The problem with that was that they were nearly an hour's drive away.

"He said he'd be right over. He was up at Sam's, already heading back down. About five minutes," the woman explained.

Carter nodded. "What's your name?"

"Jewell. Jewell Bogart."

Carter walked closer and held her hand out. "I'm Lynn Carter. I'll probably be in town a day or two. I was told there is a motel and a lodge. Any way you could find me a room for a few nights?"

Jewell shook her head. "No. Sorry."

Carter raised her eyebrows. "No?"

"They're booked up. Until September."

Carter stared at her. "You're saying there are no rooms in town?"

Jewell shrugged. "People make reservations a year in advance. Those that don't get rooms camp out in tents or bring RVs."

Carter arched an eyebrow. "So where do you suggest I stay?"

Jewell glanced behind her. "Well, the chief has a bed back there in his office, but he uses it this time of year. He's the only officer. He pretty much lives here at the station until September."

Before she could reply, the door opened. She turned, seeing a man—not much older than herself—come inside. At first glance, she didn't assume it was Chief Goodson. The man was dressed much as she was—jeans and hiking boots. The insignia on his T-shirt—and gun and holster—said otherwise, though. He gave her a friendly smile as he hurried in.

"Sorry. I was told you'd be here closer to noon." He held his hand out. "Mike Goodson." Then he frowned. "You *are* the FBI agent, right?"

She shook his hand. "Yes. Lynn Carter. I got away earlier than I expected."

"I didn't see a sheriff's department unit out front. You come up the mountain alone?"

She nodded. "I wanted a look around first."

"I see. Well, you're certainly dressed appropriately for up here. The last FBI team I worked with were all suits and ties. Of course, that was ten years ago, back when I was at LAPD."

She nodded. "Small world. I was at LAPD too. Homicide detective."

"Oh yeah? How long ago?"

"About eight months."

"I was a detective too. Worked Special Victims Unit. I doubt I know any of those guys anymore. Kinda cut ties when I left."

She nodded again. She knew that all too well. "So? Is this a good time to take a run out there?"

"Oh, sure. Makes sense, with you being a former detective and all. Nothing against those county boys in the sheriff's department, but something this gruesome, they were mostly squirming in their shoes. I imagine you'll want to look it over without an audience."

"I mostly wanted to look it over without having someone else's opinion in my ear."

"Well, I'll certainly stay out of your way, Agent Carter. Don't mind saying, it damn near gave me nightmares."

"I imagine so. I've seen the crime scene photos."

She followed him to the door, but he paused before opening it.

"Jewell, you know where I'll be. We'll probably swing by the saloon for lunch too. Want me to bring you something?"

"I'm fine. I brought leftovers from last night's dinner."

"All right. See you later."

Outside, he went toward his Jeep, motioning her to follow. "Unless you want to take yours too."

She glanced at the rental. It was an SUV, appropriate for up here, but she went around to the Jeep. "I'll ride with you. Because stopping off at a saloon later sounds like fun."

He gave a quick laugh. "Sorry. The locals still call it the saloon. It's the Timber Falls Bar and Grill. Best burgers in town. And if you hang around for dinner, the best chicken-fried steak you'll have outside of Texas." He pulled onto the road. "Are you staying overnight?"

"Don't know yet. Depends. Jewell said there were no rooms in town."

"No. They're booked. Unless there's a cancellation, but they always have a waiting list."

"What is it that people do here?"

"Run the river. Rafting. Got some nice chutes up here. Class V rapids in two places. Dead Man Falls will make you call out for Jesus when you're shooting through that one," he said with a hearty laugh. "But don't worry about housing. I've got a place going to waste. I live at the station during the summer months.

Got a little bedroom fixed up for me in the corner of my office. You're welcome to my spare room at the house. It's only a few miles out of town."

"Thanks. I appreciate that." She motioned to the shops they passed. "Is this the extent of it?"

"Mostly. This is Main Street. Got River Road on up ahead to the left. Then got a couple of raggedy side streets—Spruce and Aspen."

"Raggedy?"

"Old houses that have barely been renovated. Some of the locals live there and the others are rented out during the summer. Flip's Diner is on the corner of Aspen and River Road. If you have a hankering for pancakes, that's the place. The other eatery in town besides the saloon is the Raft House. They're only seasonal and you won't find any of the locals there."

"I see."

He laughed. "It's a small-ass town, I know, but hell, I love it."

"How did you find your way here from LA?"

He pointed as he turned onto River Road. "That's the saloon. We'll grab a burger there for lunch."

The unpaved road was aptly named as it followed the river upstream. She glanced at the building, seeing an old, faded SALOON sign hanging under the porch. The large, neat lettering on front however claimed it to be Timber Falls Bar and Grill, which she noted by another sign was NOW SERVING BREAKFAST. She spotted an outdoor patio butted up against two huge trees. The patio seemed to be hanging right over the river. Several of the tables were occupied, and she saw a yellow raft come shooting down the river.

"I got burned out on the job and went through a divorce and my life basically sucked," he said, answering her earlier question. Then he pointed to the raft with six or eight riders. "They start running the river at eight most mornings. Anyway, I grew up over in Durango. Thought I'd stay with my parents for a bit, get my head on straight. Then this little town was getting overrun with tourists and they had no police presence at all. The sheriff's department is some forty miles away, so they advertised for this position and here I am."

"You're a one-man office?"

"Me and Jewell. But she only works during the summer months. When the tourists leave in September, the shops close up and more than half the town is deserted. Not much more than a hundred of us that stay through the winter."

"Wow."

"Oh, yeah. I got a cushy job. I work my ass off all summer, then don't do a damn bit of police work the rest of the year." He laughed again. "Been here ten years. I write a few speeding tickets, break up a drunken fight now and then, and tend to fender benders on occasion. That's about it." His smile faded. "Now this. Damn. I'd forgotten what a crime scene looked like."

"What's your take on it?"

He looked at her quickly. "I thought you didn't want anyone's opinion in your ear."

She smiled at that. "We're thinking a serial killer. Do you have cause to think it might be a local? Or maybe an isolated incident?"

"Oh, hell no. It's not a goddamn local. For one thing, the average age of the locals is better than sixty-five and that's only because me and Haley bring the average down. No way a local did this."

"Haley? Your wife?"

"No, no. Haley owns the saloon. She's in her thirties. Good friend of mine. So it wasn't a local, no. I also don't think it was a one-time incident. It was too violent. There was no indication that the victim had a fight or an argument with someone. No drunken brawl. Nothing."

"Did you interview the guy who found him?"

"No. From what the campground hosts said, he was heading down to the river not long after daybreak. Saw the blood, freaked out, and ran to wake them up."

"And nothing odd or strange had happened in town? Somebody here that maybe shouldn't be?"

He slowed before turning down an even bumpier road. She saw the sign for River Road Campground, another two miles. "You're asking a lot of questions, Agent Carter. I'm fairly certain you know the sheriff's department is running this show, not me."

She nodded. "I do. Just thinking you probably have more experience at this sort of thing, that's all."

He shook his head. "Maybe ten years ago. Like I said, it's been a cushy job. Skills slip away."

"Once a cop, always a cop," she countered.

"Okay, then I'll offer this. The part of the campground where this happened—it's all college students. That's not to say that there aren't college students scattered about all over, but in this section down close to the river, all college students. That's where they stick them."

"Why's that?"

"They're noisy. They stay up late drinking. One big party."

"Okay. What's your point?"

"I did a little snooping around while I was up there." He turned into the campground, and she noted what looked like hundreds of tents spread out under the trees for as far as she could see. "Talked to David after the deputies got done with him. Asked him about this guy who reported it."

"David?"

"Campground host." He spread his hand out. "Now, as you can see, they've got a crowd here. All summer is like this, so I don't imagine he knows everyone who comes in, but he said that guy wasn't familiar. Shouldn't have even been here, he said. He was older. Not a college student."

"So you're saying that area is off-limits to others?"

"No, not at all. But at daybreak? What the hell was he doing there? There are other parts of the river to go to. Hell, they got trails going down to the water all over. Why would he be there on that particular morning—at daybreak—when he wasn't even camping in that area?"

Carter nodded but said nothing. She'd been at the crime scene in Albuquerque. Other than the hack job, the scenes weren't alike. The motel room was bloody as hell, but it hadn't been smeared all over the place like here at the campground. The injuries were similar, although the guy in the motel room hadn't been quite as brutally attacked as this guy. Although that was relative. They'd both been practically butchered. She was still waiting on the ME's report, but it was more similar than not. She hoped they would confirm the same knife was used or at least the same strike pattern.

Mike pulled to a stop and got out. "We'll have to walk from here. It's not far."

No, she could see the yellow crime scene tape from there. "Anyone stay behind to secure the area?"

"No. But let me tell you, those that were camping near him already moved on. He had three buddies with him. They packed up and left. The others close by moved farther into the woods." He shook his head. "I bet not a one of them slept a wink last night."

"So you trusted them not to trample over the scene?"

"Not me. Remember, this is the sheriff's gig, not mine. But yeah, I doubt anyone crossed the line. I'm sure some curious ones came out to take pictures. You know how people are nowadays with their damn phones. Can't look away from a train wreck."

The area did indeed seem to be isolated, and she could see the indentions on the pine needles where other tents had once stood. It wasn't quite as gruesome now. Dried blood didn't have the same effect as the freshly spilled bright red did. She lifted the crime scene tape and bent under it. Evidence markers were still on the ground, and she took care to avoid them. The tent was smeared with blood, both on the inside and out. She studied it, then motioned for Mike to join her.

"This looks staged to me."

"How so?"

She lifted the flap of the tent and peered inside. "Mostly spatter in here. Lots of it. Outside, though, it's smeared. Like the killer had blood on their hands and intentionally marked the outside of the tent."

"Why? Why chance someone seeing? Do your killing and get your ass out of there."

"Serial killers operate differently. It often becomes a game. Most think they're invincible. They're also incredibly confident. It's why they're rarely caught after only a few victims."

"You have experience?"

She nodded. "Worked one a few years back. Four victims. I did a lot of research on serial killers."

"You catch him?"

"Yeah. Took over a year, but yeah, we got him. Turned out to be the first victim's brother. The shock of it all damn near killed his mother. Good family. Normal. Middle-class."

"Never can tell."

"That's for sure." She walked around to the back of the tent. "There's even blood back here. Definitely staged."

"Knowing if it was staged or not, how does that help?"

She walked past the tent, looking at the trees closest to it. She pointed to a smudge. "Got blood here. No evidence marker."

"They mostly followed the trail to the river."

She nodded. "By staging it like this, the killer wanted to make damn sure it would be found. It also makes it a little more gruesome, as you say."

She followed the blood pattern down to the river, seeing more smears on the rocks that lined the edge. She squatted down, head tilted as she tried to imagine the killer in this same position. What had he done? Gotten into the river to wash off or just made it look that way? With as much blood that was smeared around, the killer surely would have been nearly covered in it.

She stood up, staring at the rushing water. Would he have dared venture into the river at night? It wasn't deep right along the shore, but would he have known that? She turned to Mike, who was leaning against a far tree.

"Do people get in the river here? Swim? That sort of thing?"

"Not as a rule, no. Not here, anyway. The river's got a flat stretch farther upstream. There's a park. Day use only. Fishing, mostly, but some of these kids get in. The river is tame there. Not like this."

"Cold, I imagine."

"That it is."

She pointed to where she stood. "At night, with no light, if you're the killer, are you going to get in to clean up?"

He came closer. "Unless you know what the hell you're doing, you're likely to be swept away downstream and that's all she wrote. Now these kids here, those who camp right here, they probably know this area. You've got about five feet or so where it's shallow enough. Hell, that's how most of them bathe. But at night?" He shook his head. "Can't see it. Too many rocks. Hell, it's hard enough standing upright in the daylight when the river is running this fast."

"I agree. So our killer comes to the edge, smears some blood on these rocks here," she said, pointing. "Then what?" She turned upstream. "How far is this flat stretch you're talking about?"

"Maybe a half-mile up."

She smiled at him. "Want to take a walk?"

"Nice enough day for a hike." He fell into step beside her. "When the tourists leave, me and Haley get out on the trails some. She loves to hike, does it every chance she gets. She's been all over these trails here. Me? I had turned into a city boy after all my years in LA. Took baby steps at first when it came to hiking, meaning I hardly did it. Then Haley came to town. We hit it off right away, probably because we're the youngest ones here. She drags my ass out from time to time."

"So, girlfriend then?"

"Girlfriend? No, no. I'm not Haley's type. You are, if you know what I mean," he said with a wink. "Of course, she'll tell you she's not available. She came up here to grieve." He stopped and pointed to their right. "Look there. Like someone stumbled on that rock."

She bent down, inspecting the overturned rock. "I think you're right." She put her foot where the rock was, imagining tripping on it. She looked ahead of it, seeing an indentation in the dirt. "Here. They fell here."

"Okay, I see it. So you're thinking the killer pretended to get in the river, but actually headed upstream there to where it's calm. That would mean our killer had to have known about it."

"Maybe they parked their car there. Hiked down here, went into the first tent they found."

He rubbed his chin, and it was only then that she noticed the stubble there. "These boys stay up drinking well after midnight. Chances are our victim was likely passed out or drunk. Would have been easy."

"How would our killer have known he slept alone?"

Mike grinned at her. "He did surveillance. This wasn't a crime of opportunity."

"Not likely. Which means our killer was hanging around for a day or two before the murder."

"I picture you the type who likes to work alone. And, you know, you didn't want the sheriff's deputies around. Yet you're sure asking my opinion a lot."

"I'm used to having a partner. Back at LAPD." She ran a hand over her hair, brushing it off her forehead. "I had a lot of partners, actually."

"They didn't play nice, or you didn't?"

She laughed. "They would say me." She walked on. Yeah, they would. So would her captain. She imagined the whole damn department was glad she left.

Left? Is that what she did? More like forced out. More like "This is an opportunity that will fit you perfectly, Carter." She hadn't protested much. She'd been damn tired of her picture running in the paper almost daily. Tired of the accusations, the finger pointing. Tired of being called a loose cannon. Tired of people seeing her on the street and holding their hands up. "Don't shoot! Don't shoot!"

She blew out her breath. Yeah, it was time to move on. Things had spiraled out of control there. But this new job? Hell, she wasn't even sure what she was. Her credentials said she was an FBI agent. She had yet to meet her commander. Murdock.

He was just a voice on the phone. She had no partner. She had no place to live. She had no vehicle. All her stuff was in storage, and she'd sold her car. Her first assignment had sucked. She'd flown out to Salt Lake City then rented a car. She'd spent nearly a month living in cheap motel rooms, trying to chase down a guy who had shot two tourists outside of Canyonlands National Park. While she was doing the legwork, some computer geek at Quantico was running algorithms, telling her where to look. She'd told the guy—Jason—that he was way out in left field, but damn if he hadn't finally led her right to the bastard.

It was only then that she learned she'd replaced two agents who had traveled in a motorhome, taking rural assignments. She'd also learned that Murdock had three teams and none of them were conventional. All ex-military. Which left her wondering how the hell she'd been recruited. She had no ties to the military.

"There it is," Mike said, interrupting her thoughts.

She saw a few cars parked through the trees and nodded. It was indeed like a park. Concrete picnic tables—five or six of them—were dispersed along the river. Each had a charcoal grill and a trash barrel beside it. She looked at the river, noting the smooth surface, seeing three fishermen standing up to their waists, casting fly rods.

"Trout?"

"Oh, yeah. Got nice rainbow trout here. Browns and cutthroats too." He eyed her. "You fish?"

"No. Looks like fun," she said absently as she walked along the shore. Ten steps later, she found blood. "Here."

"So our guy cleaned up here in the shallow water, then… what? Had a car stashed?"

"Probably."

"How does this help you?"

She pointed to the guys that were fishing. "Do you know them? Are they locals?"

"No, no. The locals don't venture out to the river until September when things calm down. If they fish, they go way up the mountain. There's a large creek up there—Cinnamon

Creek. Lots of nice spots to fish. Tourists don't know about it. The creek dumps into the river right above Timber Falls. Not talking about the town. The falls upstream. The town is named after them."

"Okay, so let's see if any of these guys were out here fishing in the last few days. Maybe they noticed an odd vehicle or something."

"Sure, we can ask. But look around." He motioned to the parking area. "Got eight or ten vehicles parked here. Got three guys fishing."

"So who do they belong to?"

"Hikers. Got a trail that starts at the bend there. Goes upstream a bit, then curls into a meadow. Easy hike with nice views. This time of year, lots of wildflowers. You'll have cars parked here every day."

"Okay. It won't hurt to ask, though."

That proved to be futile. This was the first day on the river for all three of them, they said.

"Let's go get a burger. I'll introduce you to Haley."

CHAPTER FOUR

Haley smiled at Mike, then arched an eyebrow as a woman followed him into the bar. An attractive woman in jeans and a black T-shirt. While her dark hair was worn short, the woman brushed at it impatiently as if it needed a cut. She moved down the bar to where they sat.

"Missed you at breakfast," she told Mike.

"Yeah, I was out early." He jerked his head toward the woman. "This here is Special Agent Carter, FBI. Carter, this is Haley Martin, my good friend."

Haley stared at the woman for a moment. While she'd never actually met an FBI agent before—or even seen one in real life—she didn't imagine this is what they looked like. This woman looked like she was perfectly at home in her jeans and hiking boots—too old to be a river rat, yet she could have easily come from one of the campgrounds. She finally held her hand out to her. "Pleased to meet you, Agent Carter."

The woman shook her hand firmly. "You can call me Carter. Everyone does."

She smiled quickly. "Hate your first name, do you?"

The woman smiled back at her. "Not really, no. It's Lynn. I've been in law enforcement since I was twenty-one. So it's just Carter."

"Sure. If that's what you wish." She glanced at Mike. "You want tea?"

Mike nodded. "Supposed to meet a couple of the sheriff's deputies up here around noon. Since I missed breakfast, thought we could squeeze in a burger. I told Carter you made the best."

Haley nodded. "Wait until she tastes the steak fries." She looked at Carter. "You'll be spoiled after that." She took out a pad, scribbling down Mike's order. Cheeseburger, no pickles. Extra fries. She looked questioningly at the FBI agent. "How would you like yours?"

"What are my choices?"

"Oh. Sorry." She pulled out a menu from under the bar. "I prefer the Dead Man's burger, with mushrooms and jack. If you're daring, the Timber burger has two patties."

"Dead Man's burger?"

"Named after the rapids south of town."

"I see. Well, I do love mushrooms. I guess I'll give it a try. And your famous steak fries, of course."

Mike gave her a wink as she took the order to Sylvia in the kitchen. She knew what that wink was. He often did that when a cute woman came to the bar. She hadn't told him much about Gail—or her personal life, for that matter—but he knew enough to know that she was not in the least bit interested in any sort of romantic—or physical—relationship. Just the thought of being with someone else, someone other than Gail, made her nearly cringe.

Their relationship had been so perfect, she couldn't imagine spoiling the memory of that. They'd met at eighteen, both just starting their college careers. There was no instant attraction and teenage lust, no. They'd fallen into a fast friendship, a friendship that grew into more that first summer when Gail had invited her up here to Timber Falls to run the river. At the time, she had no idea what "run the river" meant, but by then, she'd wanted to spend every waking hour with Gail, so she'd ditched her summer job—and her parents—to spend two months on the river. And by the end of summer, she was madly in love. When she'd taken Gail home to meet the family, the sudden shock— "Yes, I'm gay and this is my girlfriend"—subsided quickly as Gail's vibrant personality won over her parents in record time.

She sighed, feeling that very fleeting happiness that came to her when she let in those early memories of Gail. Yes, fleeting. Because the happiness was always replaced with reality. Gail was gone.

"Two burgers," she said, placing the order next to the griddle where Sylvia liked it. "Mike's usual and a Dead Man's."

"Who's the gal with him? Doesn't seem his type."

She laughed. "Does Mike have a type?"

The older woman laughed lightly. "Now that he's forty, I suppose he's outgrown the river rats."

"I'll say. But that woman is an FBI agent."

Sylvia looked at her sharply. "FBI? Because of the killing?"

"Yes."

"Well, I'll tell you, Herbie slept with his rifle next to our bed last night." Then she chuckled. "He's eighty-two. I told him if someone broke into the house, by the time he got his rickety old body out of bed, we'd both be dead." She laughed again. "Takes him ten minutes just to sit up." Then her smile faded. "Horrible thing, that poor boy. His parents are probably beside themselves."

"Yes, I'm sure they are." She patted Sylvia's hand. "Let's hope the killer is long gone from here now."

Of course, she didn't know if that was the case or not. She went back out, knowing she could ask Mike any question point-blank. But he might be a little more guarded with the FBI here and all. She decided she didn't care. She filled two glasses with ice, then topped them off with tea before bringing them to the bar.

"So what's the word? Are we in danger?"

"Who knows?" Mike shrugged. "Carter here is sharp though. Found where the killer cleaned up. Over at the park."

"I thought there was already a trail going right to the river."

"It was staged," Carter supplied. Then she looked at Mike. "You often discuss open cases with the locals?"

Mike laughed. "We don't have open cases in Timber Falls, as a rule. Besides, if we don't tell them, rumors will run amok. I'd rather have everything out in the open. Of course, I don't really have any say in this, I suppose. Not my deal."

Haley looked pointedly at Agent Carter then. "So?"

"So?"

"Should we be worried?"

"Too early to tell, really. If it's a random killing then, yes, I'd be concerned. Lock your doors at night, for sure."

She let out a breath. "I was kinda hoping you'd say no. I'm living here above the bar for the next few days, so I guess I feel safer here than at home where I'd be alone." At Carter's blank expression, she continued, "My seasonal workers live here. I have housing upstairs. Well, four small rooms that they share but still, safety in numbers and all that."

"I think we'll—" Mike started but his phone interrupted. He glanced at it, then at Agent Carter. "The boys from down the mountain. Probably looking for you." He answered, his voice turning professional again. "Chief Goodson here."

Haley smiled at him, then slid her gaze to Carter. She knew Mike well and the tone and manner of his conversation with Agent Carter indicated that he thought of her as more friend than colleague, which was strange considering they'd only met that morning. She tuned out Mike's conversation, meeting the woman's friendly gaze instead.

"How long will you be in town?"

"Don't know yet. Depends on our killer, I guess." Then she leaned closer, a bit of a flirty smile on her face. "Why? Are you offering…companionship if I stay a night or two?"

Haley nearly gasped. *"What?"* Then she took a step away. "Seriously?"

Agent Carter laughed. "What? Too forward?"

"You think?"

"I thought I'd give it a try, even though Mike says you're unavailable."

"Is that what he says?"

"Is he wrong?"

Haley shook her head. "No. No, he's not wrong. Sorry. I'm not available. And not interested. At all."

Carter was still smiling. "Sorry then. Been on the road for about eight months now. You're the very first woman I've flirted with, and you certainly put me in my place."

Before she could reply, Mike pocketed his phone. "They're already heading to the scene. Didn't find me at the station and assumed I'd hauled you out there. They seemed a little peeved that you'd come up early without them."

"Don't care."

"No, don't imagine that you do. Unless, of course, you need backup for something."

Agent Carter clapped his shoulder. "That's what I've got you for."

"Yeah. I was afraid you were going to say that."

Haley again noticed the easy camaraderie between them. "You want to take your burgers with you?"

"No, hell, I told them we were grabbing an early lunch. Told them we'd meet them out there in about thirty minutes. Weren't none too pleased." He took a big swallow of his tea. "Gonna let Carter here stay at my house while she's in town."

Haley's eyebrows shot up. "Really?"

"Where else is she going to stay? No rooms in town. Unless you want to offer the apartment upstairs."

"Which would be fine except that I'm staying there this week." The bell dinged in the serving window, and she turned, seeing two plates with burgers and steak fries. "Your order is up."

So Agent Carter would be staying at Mike's place while she was in town. She wondered if she'd still be there by Saturday when she moved back into her own house. She and Mike lived within walking distance through the forest. She supposed she would feel safer knowing there was an FBI agent nearby. That thought, of course, made her sad. She'd never once, in all these years, felt anything other than safe here in tiny Timber Falls.

CHAPTER FIVE

Carter sat up with a start, feeling disoriented. She blinked her eyes, listening, but heard nothing. She lay back down, her eyes staring into the darkness. Eight months since she'd slept in her own bed. She never knew where the hell she was when she woke up. Mike Goodson's spare room this time.

For some reason, she'd taken an instant liking to the man. While he pretended to be an out-of-touch police officer just killing time up here, his eyes were sharp, and she imagined his instincts were as well. Three deputies had made the trip up to meet her, but she'd learned more from reading the file than from them. She toured the area with them again and took a few pictures of the scene. They then took the tent down, folding it up neatly into a large evidence bag. The physical items inside the tent had been taken the day before, sent on to the regional forensic lab.

She rolled over, wondering what Murdock expected her to do up here. Based on the smear marks, the killer had worn gloves. There would be no prints found, same as the first killing.

She had yet to get results from the lab. At least the same lab would be going over both scenes. Hopefully they would come up with something. The forensics team in Albuquerque had been thorough, and she'd already gotten their initial report. They collected stray fibers and hair at the motel room, but it was an ancient, not particularly well-kept place. The likelihood that any evidence pointed to their killer was slim. The place hadn't exactly been immaculate.

She rolled over again, feeling restless. She reached out for her phone. It was twenty minutes until five. She closed her eyes for a second, feeling a wave of loneliness wash over her. A big, heavy wave at that. It had been happening more and more lately, and she realized she probably wasn't cut out for this—this job that had her traveling around by herself, meeting people on the fly, learning to trust strangers and make a new friend for a day or two.

She didn't know why she was feeling lonely, really. It wasn't like she left behind a huge circle of friends. Even on the force, she hadn't been that close with anyone. Partners came and went frequently, it seemed.

And personally? Well, there was Darla. She supposed what they'd been doing for the last few years would be called dating. Darla saw others, though, she knew that. She didn't really care. Darla was someone to be with on those occasions when she needed someone. There was no deep emotional attachment, no tears when she left, no sense of loss. For either of them.

Yet now, here in this strange bed, she was feeling lonely. She didn't know what direction her life was taking. Hell, she didn't even know where she wanted to go. For that matter, she didn't know how she'd gotten there in the first place. The last few months of her police career seemed to blur together—the investigation, the accusations, the guilt, the self-doubt, the very public scrutiny. Thoughts of quitting were coupled with the fear of getting fired. Or worse.

Sometimes she just wanted to throw in the towel and walk away. Other times, she wanted to fight for the career she loved. It wasn't until her captain had called her in and she had assumed it was all over with that she took a true assessment of her feelings. He had taken the decision out of her hands. Because at that moment, she wasn't sure if she still loved the job or not. Didn't matter. A conference call with a man named Murdock had her on a plane to Phoenix within a week, with freshly minted FBI credentials. She worked with Special Agent Reynolds and his team for nearly a month, learning the ropes of this new gig she had. Reynolds was a stickler for rules and protocol. It was only by a sheer force of will that she made the month without coming to blows with him.

Now she was running solo, heading off to wherever Murdock sent her, putting out fires big and small. Mostly small. She was eight months in now, and she was still trying to find her way. Nothing like a serial killer to make her take stock of her life.

With a sigh, she sat up and rubbed her eyes. Yeah, it had been a whirlwind, yet time seemed to tick by ever so slowly. She hadn't even let her family know that she'd left. Had they missed her?

"Probably not," she murmured to the dark room.

No, she doubted her parents gave her much thought. Nothing had changed in that regard. She was still the forgotten middle child. She wasn't their handsome baby boy with blue eyes, the oldest of the three of them. Nor was she the little princess that Laurel had been. Still was a princess, she supposed. She didn't know why they'd never coddled her as they had Reggie and Laurel. She couldn't even blame it on her being gay or on her profession. No, their indifference to her had started well before then. When had she first felt the abandonment? At eight? Ten?

Before she could delve into *that* subject, she stood and made her way down the hallway and into the spare bathroom. No, she didn't dwell on it much anymore. She was the black sheep of the family but not by her choosing. Of course, at times she was happy for that. The other two had been pampered and protected and bailed out of more jams than she could count. They never learned life's hard lessons, never learned how to pick themselves up after a fall. Never learned the value of a dollar.

They were weak where she was strong. For that, she could be grateful that her parents had let her find her own way without their interference.

She splashed water on her face, then stared into the mirror. She sometimes didn't recognize herself. It wasn't just her aging face—creases around her eyes that only a few years ago hadn't been there. It wasn't the creases, no, but the eyes themselves. They seemed blank, expressionless—empty. Empty of life, of love. Empty of emotion. That look frightened her sometimes. Like now, wondering who it was she was looking back at.

She looked away from the mirror, pulling her T-shirt over her head instead. She stepped quickly into the shower, not caring in the least that the water was just this side of freezing.

At least it made her feel something.

CHAPTER SIX

It was early—not yet six—as she drove down River Road toward the tiny village of Timber Falls. The sky was showing signs of morning even though the mountain would hide the sun for another hour, she supposed. As she passed the campgrounds, people were starting to stir. There was still a chill in the air, and she couldn't imagine getting out on the river this early. Mike had told her last night that the first run of the day started about eight, downstream from the waterfalls—Timber Falls—that the town was named after. The river plunged forty feet there at the falls, but even then, "idiots" tried to kayak them. In his ten years here, they'd had six drownings up at the falls, he'd said.

The outfitters in town did raft tours all day, the last stopping about three. Those that started below the falls took six to seven hours to reach the last take-out point before the river became too treacherous again. Along that stretch of waterway, rafters would encounter six nice rapids, including the Class V Dead Man Falls, just downstream of town. He'd made it sound so exciting, she'd wanted to sign up for a trip herself. The morning, though, brought reality. She was working. No time for a tour of the river.

She slowed as she approached town, glancing toward the saloon, surprised to see lights on inside. She pulled up, wondering if Haley was open already or just readying things for breakfast. The saloon had been busy last night and even though she and Mike sat at the bar, they hadn't had much of a chance to visit with her. She had learned that Haley's morning staff had quit on her, and she was covering as both waitress and cook for the week until one of her seasonal workers changed shifts. She hadn't thought to ask what time she started serving breakfast.

As she walked up to the door, she saw the CLOSED sign still hanging there. In the window was another sign. HELP WANTED. She stared at it for a second, then tried the door. It was unlocked so she went inside. A bell jingled, announcing her presence.

"Be with you in a second," Haley called from the kitchen. "Grab any table you like."

Instead of a table, she went up to the bar, then through the opening that led to the kitchen. She leaned against the doorway, watching as Haley took a large slab of bacon from the fridge and placed it beside the griddle, which appeared to be hot and sizzling already. When Haley turned, she visibly jumped when she saw her.

"Sorry," Carter said automatically.

Haley took a deep breath, then smiled. "Good morning, Agent Carter. And yes, you startled me. Want some coffee?"

"Please."

She went back out, this time taking a proper seat at the bar. Haley filled two cups, bringing one to her. It was then that Carter noticed the ring on her left hand—a gold band. A wedding ring?

"You're out and about early. Leaving town already?"

She took two packets of sugar and added it to her coffee. "Not unless there's another killing. I'll probably hang out here until I get the lab results." She took a sip and nodded. "This is good. Not your usual cheap diner coffee."

Haley laughed lightly at that. "The first pot is the good stuff. I usually drink half of it before anyone comes in, unless Mike pops over early." She pointed to the setup behind the bar. There were two pots warming. "That's your cheap diner coffee."

"Closed sign is still up, but your door was unlocked. Habit?"

Haley nodded. "When Curtis and Molly lived upstairs, they'd come down about five to get everything ready, then drink coffee, waiting on the first customer. We officially open at six, but they always unlocked the door by a quarter 'til."

"And you're living here now?"

"Just until Saturday. One of my nighttime seasonals has agreed to switch to mornings." She held her hand up. "I know what you're thinking. I'm the boss and I should be able to switch their hours at will." She shook her head. "That's not how it works. I advertise for certain time slots, and they apply to which slot fits their needs. CeCe has been with me three years—this will be her last—and with a little coaxing and bribery—I gave her the week off with pay—she's switching from nights to mornings starting on Sunday."

"Why her last?"

"She graduated. She's got a tech job lined up in San Francisco starting in September."

"Is it stressful having to rely on seasonal workers?"

"Very, although I've been lucky for the most part. In the seven years I've owned the place, there have only been a few I'd rather toss back." Haley reached for the coffeepot and topped off both their cups. "Because I can provide housing, most who work one year want to come back the next so that makes it a bit easier."

She added another packet of sugar to her cup. "So, what's your story?"

Haley's eyebrows shot up. "My story?"

"Yeah. What brought you to this little town?" She gave a quick smile. "You do consider it a town, right?"

Haley smiled too. "It feels much larger in the summer than winter. In fact, it was quite a thriving town back in the 1800s. Silver. There were several mines in the mountains here. River

Road used to be quite notorious, I'm told. Several hotels and saloons. Most were brothels. There was a huge fire, though. This saloon and a few odd buildings were the only ones that survived along River Road. The town sort of fizzled out then, as did the mines. It wasn't until the late 1970s that rafting took hold up here." She took a sip of her coffee and smiled. "Tidbits I've learned from the locals. I'm certainly no expert on the history of Timber Falls. I first came here the summer of my freshman year in college."

"Were you one of those river rats, as Mike calls them?"

"I was." The wistful look on Haley's face lingered, as if she was thinking back to that time in her life. Then she pushed it away with a forced smile. "Came here every summer. Fell in love for the first time up here." The forced smile disappeared. "The only time."

Carter looked pointedly at the ring on her finger. Haley followed her gaze, then the fingers of her right hand automatically found the band, twisting it several times.

"I...I was married."

Carter nodded. "She gone?" When Haley stared at her, eyebrow raised, she continued, "Mike said you'd come up here to grieve. He didn't elaborate."

The front door opened, and the bell jingled, signaling a customer. Carter watched as Haley transformed her face, smiling brightly and offering a cheery greeting. She wondered if they could tell it was forced.

"Take any table you want. Coffee?"

"Oh, please."

Haley looked at her, meeting her gaze for a second. Her eyes were a pretty mix of blue and green. "Be right back."

She took the pot of diner coffee and two menus. Carter looked up into the mirror behind the bar, watching as Haley filled their cups. She couldn't quite hear their conversation. She let her eyes linger. Haley's hair was more blond than brown, more straight than wavy, reaching just past her shoulders in the back. The sides were cut a little shorter, and Haley had the strands tucked behind her ears. She was attractive and pleasant as was evidenced by her interaction with her customers. Yet there was an aloofness to her, a façade, as if she were playing a part, showing only the briefest of glimpses into who she really was. Yes, she'd noticed that yesterday when they'd first met. Haley had been friendly, yet distant—guarded. But what was she protecting? Her past? Her future?

"More coffee or did you come for breakfast?"

Carter nodded. "Both. I'm surprised I'm hungry after eating that steak last night."

Haley took the pot of "good" coffee from the warmer and added to her cup. "It was good, right? Curtis said anyone can make a chicken-fried steak, but the secret to making a good one was the seasoning in the batter."

"It was delicious, yes. You mentioned Curtis and Molly. There's a help wanted sign out front. I take it they're not here any longer?"

"No. They were with me since the beginning. Molly's mother is having some health issues, so they moved back to be with her. Depending on how that turns out, they may return. I hope so. I relied on them for so much. Now that they're gone, I realize I didn't pay them nearly enough."

"They lived upstairs?"

"Yes. I could count on them to run the place for me. They were older, responsible. And while I trust the ones I've got working here now, they're not invested in anything. They're just college students looking to have a good summer. With Curtis and Molly gone, I've got to be here a lot more and it's already wearing on me. I'm exhausted."

"No free time, huh?"

"None whatsoever." She pulled out a menu from under the bar. "Here. It's your basic breakfast fare."

She walked off, back to the table to take their order. The bell jingled again, and another couple came in. Before the door closed on them, three yawning young men walked in, nearly stumbling to a nearby table. Haley greeted them all with a cheerful "Good morning." Carter wondered how she was going to manage this many breakfast orders by herself.

CHAPTER SEVEN

Haley took three slices of bacon, listening to the familiar sizzle as she placed them on the hot griddle. Two sausage patties joined them, and she let them cook for a bit before moving them over. She cracked four eggs, then added more bacon grease as Curtis had taught her. She got the hash browns on the griddle next, then took out four slices of bread, intending to toast them in butter. She wasn't a pro, and she didn't have her timing down yet, but she'd grown by leaps and bounds in the last week. This morning, however, would be a challenge. The bell jingled yet again, signaling new arrivals. Well, they'd have to wait. She'd learned from experience—and burnt bacon and overcooked eggs—not to leave the griddle unattended.

"Need some help?"

She glanced up, finding Carter leaning in the doorway much as she'd been earlier that morning.

"Can you cook?"

Carter came closer. "Enough to know that those eggs need to be flipped."

"Great! You're hired." She shoved the spatula into her hands. "Add more bacon grease around the eggs. It helps prevent the yolk from breaking when you turn them." She plopped butter onto the griddle next. "Once you flip the eggs, add the bread on top of the butter. Be right back."

She grabbed the coffeepot as she went out, smiling at anyone who looked her way. "Coffee?" she asked to no one in particular.

She placed menus on the table of four who had just come in and filled three cups. The other wanted orange juice only. She took two orders from other tables and hurried back into the kitchen, hoping that Carter hadn't made a mess of things. Quite the opposite, in fact. She had two plates already ready to go.

"Took a chance on the servings. Bacon, two eggs, toast. Sausage, two eggs, toast. Hash browns on each. Right?"

"Perfect." She slapped down the two new orders with a grin. "I think I might keep you." She went back out with the plates, going to the first table. "Here you go. Anything else?"

"No, we're good. Thanks."

"Great. Enjoy."

Before she made it back to the bar, the bell jingled again, and she sighed. What was going on this morning? But it was Mike who came in, and she gave him a friendly smile.

"Good morning," she greeted.

He looked around with raised eyebrows. "You got a breakfast sale going on or something?" he teased.

"I know. And if not for my unexpected help this morning, I'd be pulling my hair out about now." She filled him a mug as he sat down at the bar. "Let me check on her."

"Her who?"

"Carter." Mike's eyebrows shot up and Haley nodded. "Yeah, she's pretty handy in the kitchen."

So much so that Carter had the eggs and bacon sizzling in unison with bread standing by ready to go.

"This is making me hungry."

"You're doing a *great* job," she said enthusiastically. "Keep it up and you'll get a raise."

Carter laughed. "Are you flirting with me?"

Haley was taken aback, but only for a second. Had she ever been accused of flirting with anyone? *Was* she flirting? God, of course not. She shook her head. "I was thinking of food. Like, breakfast is on the house."

To which Carter laughed again. "I would hope so, considering I'll most likely be cooking it."

Haley nudged her. "Flip those already. And Mike is here. Do you have some police stuff to talk about?"

"I don't think so. I'm waiting on lab reports." She carefully flipped all four eggs, the yolks still intact. "Oh, and this one has a taco. Chorizo. Where's that?"

Haley went to the fridge and pulled out the container of Mexican sausage. She scooped out a generous portion and put it on the griddle, away from the bacon. "Scramble the eggs for the taco."

"In what?"

"I just crack them on the griddle and scramble them with the spatula as they cook. Put some bacon grease down first."

Carter plated the eggs that she'd just flipped and slid them over to her. Haley put the toast down, watching as Carter cracked two more eggs.

"This can't be healthy."

"What's that?"

"All this bacon grease," Carter said as she scrambled the eggs.

Haley flipped the toast over, then plated the bacon and hash browns. "As Curtis would say, that's what makes it good." She took the toast off then nudged Carter again. "Stir the chorizo." She went to the fridge to get a tortilla and she tossed that on the griddle as well. "Just between you and me, I don't normally eat here. Well, I do this week since I've been staying here, but normally I eat oatmeal and fruit. Or I'll do a green smoothie or something."

"I used to make green smoothies too—throw a scoop of protein powder in there and hit the gym." Carter sighed. "Back when I had a life."

Haley wanted to ask more, but the bell jingled yet again and the plates were ready to serve. "Add a little cheese to the taco. It's in the fridge. I'll be back to get it in a sec."

She hurried out, still wondering at Carter's comment. Did she have demons in her past too? That thought made her stop in her tracks. *Too?* She certainly didn't have demons. What she carried with her—Gail—wasn't something that haunted her. She kept Gail close because she wanted to. That was her choice. There were no *demons* to fight. No.

CHAPTER EIGHT

"Surveillance? Murdock, I'm lucky to have cell service. This is in the middle of the proverbial nowhere." She looked over at Mike, who was fiddling with his computer. "The local police chief has been helpful, though." Mike looked up and grinned.

"Give everything you get to Jason. Let him run whatever algorithms he's got."

"Yeah, so like the last time I worked with Jason, I feel kinda like a puppet out here. And kinda stupid when I talk to him. To be honest with you, I don't even know what the hell I'm supposed to be doing." She walked down the hallway a bit, giving herself some privacy. "I mean, I have credentials that say I'm an FBI agent, but…am I?"

"Look, I know you just got thrown out there. You spent a month with Reynolds and his team, but going out on your own is not the same. I know that. But when Agents Ross and Sullivan quit on me, I had to scramble and, well, you were it."

"Why? Why me?" She was surprised that question was met with a laugh.

"Dare I say you reminded me of Cameron Ross? Or maybe Sullivan. She came from LAPD too. I needed someone who wasn't afraid to buck the system. Someone who wasn't afraid to take chances. Yet someone I could trust to do the job the right way. I had feelers out in a lot of the major police departments. Your captain gave you high marks."

"My captain wanted to get rid of me."

"No doubt. And while the reasons may have been warranted—and politically motivated—for LAPD, those same reasons made you attractive to me."

"I learned from Reynolds that your teams are ex-military."

"As a rule. But the personalities and the skill set that I covet don't grow on trees, Agent Carter. For your purposes, though, I needed an agent who could replace Ross and Sullivan in the short term. As you know, they operated out of a motorhome and took rural assignments. I hope to have that motorhome staffed and on the road again within the year. It started out as a solo job. I think that's how I'd like to continue it. And now, after eight months of working with you, I think I'd like you to be that agent to take over. But it involves more than field work. It means working closely with Jason and getting some training from him on how to run his algorithms. It took Cameron a while to get on board with it, but once she did, she embraced it. I hope you'll feel the same way."

"So, keep the same routine? Feed Jason the forensic reports, the lab reports, and let him tell me what to do?"

"Work any physical evidence as you see fit, Carter. But yes, feed everything you have to Jason. He's great at establishing a pattern. Trust him."

She sighed. "Okay."

"Great. Now I need to run. I'll try to schedule some time so we can have a lengthy video chat. I know this is unorthodox, Carter. But that's just the way it is."

"I guess I've gotten used to it."

"We'll talk soon."

The line went dead, and she pocketed her phone. Did she want to be that person? That person who worked alone, traveled alone? In a damn motorhome? While she wouldn't say she was a particularly gregarious person, she still liked to be around people. Sometimes. After eight months of living—and working—solo, fingers of loneliness were starting to pick at her. Maybe it was living in nameless motel rooms. Maybe it was flying here and there and not having any roots. Would living in a motorhome change that?

"Everything okay?"

She turned, finding Mike leaning against the wall, watching her. "My boss. Going over my job description."

"Oh? Is this your first gig?"

"No."

He shoved off the wall. "No. Didn't think so. You said you'd left LAPD eight months ago. I assume that meant you'd been with the FBI that long."

"I have. Let's just say it wasn't a planned career move." She cleared her throat. "So, any news?"

"Not officially, no. I'm not really in the loop. But I did hear from Bob Randal earlier. He's one of the deputies. We get along well. Anyway, he said they found a book inside the tent."

"A book?"

"Yeah. You know, they took all the stuff in the tent the day they took the body. Anyway, he said it's a kid's book. But guess what? The same book was found in the motel room in Albuquerque."

She nodded, remembering that from the report. She'd dismissed it as incidental. "So the killer wanted to make damn sure we knew he did both murders What was the name of the book?"

"Oh, hell, I don't know. He didn't say."

"Probably doesn't matter, but I know Jason will ask."

"Who's Jason?"

"He's the computer genius I work with. Every bit of information, no matter how insignificant, goes into some algorithm he wrote."

"How does that help?"

"It's about establishing a pattern, and with enough information, he can determine the killer's next move, probably before the killer has even thought about it." She held her hand up when he would have asked more questions. "It's way over my head. But he's been right more often than not."

"So, say you didn't have the killing in Albuquerque, we just had this one. And say the killer skips town and is never heard from again. Then what?"

"Yeah, that's a problem. There isn't enough information for him to input. In that case, it's old-fashioned police work."

"Talk to witnesses, hope you get a print, that sort of thing."

He nodded. "And we got nothing on that front."

"Don't discount the lab. Even if our killer was wearing gloves, such violent attacks with a knife, maybe he cut himself. Maybe we'll get a hair sample or maybe our victims fought back, and we'll get skin cells under their nails. We might get lucky and get DNA. Even luckier, might get a hit in the system."

"Well, I don't know about the scene in Albuquerque, but this one? Whoever did this, they've killed before."

"I agree. That's something else Jason will do. Run our findings through the FBI database and see if there's a similar match. Serial killers don't always keep to a timeline. They may kill, then lay low and fade back into society for years before something triggers them to kill again."

Mike led them back into his office. "You were at the saloon early. Before six, Haley said. Early riser or did you not sleep well?"

She sat down across from his desk and crossed her legs, resting an ankle on her knee. "Slept fine, thanks. I guess. I never know where the hell I am when I wake up."

"No home?"

"No. I've been on the road the whole time."

"Damn, that would suck."

"Yeah, it does." She twisted the lace of her boot between her fingers. "What's your normal day like?"

"This time of year? I mostly drive up and down the river. Make a swing through the campgrounds a couple of times. I help out some at the last take-out spot. Just have a presence around, you know."

"How long are the river trips? I know you said the long one was six or seven hours."

"Varies. The long one starts up below Timber Falls and goes down nearly twenty miles. Yeah, that takes the good part of the day. There are four different put-in spots. The two outfitters here on the river manage the put-in and take-out spots. For the most part, their guides are experienced, and we don't normally have any problems. Although the rafts get flipped on a regular basis going through Dead Man Falls. Especially early in the season when the river is flowing at a good pace. A lot of beginners will skip that. They'll put in downstream of the falls. Pretty tame after that with only a few spots that'll get your adrenaline going. That's the short three-hour trip."

"And everyone does one a day? Or they stay a week or what?"

"Some of them stay a month, but that doesn't mean they run the river every day. Most of them are college students and they can't afford it. The tamer part of the river—up by the park where we went yesterday and down below Dead Man's—gets some kayak use. The outfitters will rent those too. And some brave souls will attempt to kayak the whole damn thing."

"Do you act as search and rescue too?"

"On occasion. The county has a SAR team, though."

"That's a lot going on for just one man."

He nodded but gave an easy smile. "Like I said, it's only a few months. September into April is my free time. Can't complain about the job one bit. I feel damn lucky to have it. Now granted, the pay wouldn't feed a family of six, but hell, I've got everything I need. Wouldn't trade it for a million bucks, I'll tell you that, Carter. To me, this is heaven. I found my peace right here."

She wondered what that would feel like. Her job in LA was fast-paced and stressful. There was never any peace. And now, as she flitted about from state to state, town to town, peace was elusive as well. Of course, she wasn't really searching for peace, was she?

Perhaps that's why she hadn't found it. She hadn't known to look for it.

CHAPTER NINE

Haley wasn't surprised this time when Carter came in at a quarter to six. She poured her a cup of coffee and slid it to the edge of the bar before she'd even sat down.

"Missed you last night for dinner. Thought maybe you'd skipped town without saying goodbye."

Carter shook her head as she grabbed two sugar packets. "Would you have missed me if I had?"

"Well, I would have missed your cooking, that's for sure."

Carter gave her a quick smile. "See? I'm growing on you. But no, I was down the mountain, meeting with the sheriff's deputies. Then spent a couple of hours with the forensic team at the lab."

"Where is that?"

"There's a regional crime lab that's shared between New Mexico and Colorado. It's just across the border."

"Guess you got back late then."

"Just now, in fact." She took a sip of her coffee. "Thanks. I needed that."

"Surely you haven't been up all night."

Carter met her gaze and smiled. "Are you worried about me?"

Haley rolled her eyes. "Can't I say anything without you assuming I'm flirting with you?"

"I haven't been flirted with in so long, I guess I've forgotten the cues. And no, I haven't been up all night. Drove up early. I thought you might need help with the breakfast crowd again this morning, that's all."

Haley found herself smiling at her. "That was sweet of you. Are you *sure* you're an FBI agent?"

"What? We can't be thoughtful?"

Haley added a little coffee to her own cup. "Any news?"

Carter shook her head. "Not really. They determined that a different knife was used, but the strike patterns seemed to match. And they found a book at both scenes."

"That's what Mike said."

"It's an old children's book. Originally published back in 1992."

"Is this where you go and track down who purchased the books recently?"

Carter smiled at her. "It's actually still in print. Hop on Amazon and you can have it delivered in two days."

"So can you find out who bought copies of it?"

Carter shook her head. "It's a popular series apparently. They're available everywhere. This one is called *Alone With the Bears*. They're all outdoor adventure stories with different kids each time. And yes, I ordered a book."

"To see if there's a clue or something inside?"

Carter laughed. "You watch too much TV."

"I watch no TV. I don't even own one."

"Really?"

"When I moved here, I…" She paused, knowing whatever she let slip out would garner more questions. Carter had asked her yesterday what her story was. Did she want to share that?

"You moved here what?" Carter prompted.

Haley let out a breath. "Gail had died, and I was just going through the motions in my job. I up and quit one day with nothing to fall back on." How did she explain the compulsion she had to come to Timber Falls? "When we were in college, we came up here each summer. It was such a happy, carefree time and I was feeling lost and alone and…" She shrugged. "I came up here planning to stay a week and just reconnect with… with myself, really. And with Gail. It was early September and the river had slowed. I came here to the saloon. Sat right down there at the bar." She pointed to the spot that Butter Bill normally occupied. "Eddie and Charlotte owned it then. They wanted to retire and head down to Florida. Long story short, my grandmother loaned me the money to buy it."

"Spur-of-the-moment decision?"

Haley laughed. "Very. And I bought it right at the end of tourist season. It was just a bar then that only served crappy burgers and wings. I spent the whole first winter getting it fixed up into a real restaurant. By the time the season started up again, I was open for breakfast and lunch too. And I was in *way* over my head."

"In walked Curtis?"

"Yes. He and Molly saved me, no doubt. I let them move into the apartment upstairs and I bunked with Mike. Of course, like now, he slept at the station during the summer, so I had his house to myself." She held her hand up. "Sorry, I'm taking the long way around on this story. I—"

"Tell me about Gail."

Haley stared at her. "What do you want to know?"

"You met in college, fell in love up here, got married. Then what?"

"We…we moved to Denver." She shrugged. "Normal life, really. We liked the same things for the most part." She looked away. "Except for one. She was an avid hiker." She shook her head quickly. "Not to imply that I don't like to hike. I do. In fact, it was something we did most weekends to get out of the city. We would pack a lunch and do a three- or four-hour hike, then head back. That turned out to be too tame for her. She liked to hike to the top of mountains. Really, really tall mountains. She had a couple of buddies that she started going with. During the summer, they'd be out on the trail before daybreak most weekends. Hike ten or twelve hours to the peak and back. That was her passion. I went with them one time, thinking I might like it as much, but I found it wasn't for me."

She picked up the coffeepot and realized her hand was shaking. She spilled a little as she refilled their cups. "She...she fell to her death," she said quietly, the words seeming to hang in the air. "On one of those hikes, she slipped and...and—"

"How old were you?"

"Twenty-six. It happened in early June, and I moved up here in January."

"And you came without a TV?"

Haley smiled and nodded, remembering why she was telling this story in the first place. "Yes. I needed time to reflect on my life and come to terms with Gail's death and I didn't want any distractions. Still don't."

Carter met her gaze. "Mike said you still grieve."

Haley took a deep breath. "I guess I do. She's not ever very far away." Out of habit, she spun the wedding band on her finger. "If you're wondering, I live a solitary life by choice. Gail was everything to me and my heart shattered when she died." She forced a smile to her face. "I don't suppose it will ever heal and that's okay. I've embraced my life as it is now. I'm okay with being alone. It's by choice," she said again, not knowing if it was Carter she was trying to convince or herself.

Before Carter could reply, the front door opened, the jingle of the bell shattering the early morning quiet. Out of habit, she smiled and nodded at the customers, a young man and two women.

"Good morning. Take any table you like." She picked up the coffeepot, then looked back at Carter. "You going to hang around?"

Carter nodded. "Yeah. I'll help you cook."

CHAPTER TEN

"It's a children's book." She held her cell phone to her ear as she paced across Mike's back deck. "I don't know if it's significant or not, but I ordered the damn thing. I'll give it a read."

"What does Jason say?"

"Jason doesn't say anything unless his computer tells him to." She paused at the railing, looking out into the darkness. "The lab said they'd have the tox report back on our first victim tomorrow and, with luck, a preliminary one on victim two. The ME confirmed the strike patterns on the knife are the same, but different knives were used. Hayden Anderson, vic two, was killed with a longer knife. The blade is estimated to be ten inches long. Vic number one was six inches."

"What about surveillance at the motel in Albuquerque?" Murdock asked. "I know you said the camera wasn't functional, but what about surrounding buildings?"

"It's in an older part of town, off the beaten path. The local police pulled the video feed from a used car lot that is just down the road. Not sure what good that will do, but they're going over it. The victim checked in before six o'clock, alone. Had a pizza delivered at 7:04. The police spoke with the delivery guy. He said our victim was alone and nothing seemed out of the ordinary."

"And no neighbors heard anything or saw anything."

"Right. Estimated time of death—two a.m."

"Okay. Where are you anyway? Did you go back to Albuquerque?"

"I'm actually in Timber Falls."

"I thought they'd cleared that scene."

She nodded into the darkness. "Yeah, they did. Thought I'd hang out here until we have something. The police chief is letting me bunk at his house."

"Okay, well, do what you want. What about the sheriff's department? You getting any pushback from them?"

"None. I think they're glad to have me here."

"They've probably not ever worked a serial killer. For them, it's just one victim, though. We've had cases like this before. Several. They sometimes drag out for months."

"Yeah. I actually worked one in LA a few years ago. Took a year and four victims to catch him."

"Let's hope this one won't be a repeat of that. Use Jason as much as you can. I'll be in touch."

As she'd learned in the last eight months, Murdock rarely ended his calls with pleasantries. She pocketed her phone, then leaned on the railing. The back porch deck was quite large and hung over the side of the hill some fifteen feet from the ground. The front deck was smaller and on ground level. It was nice too, but there was no view. The back deck looked out toward the river and town. Not that there was a view at this time of night. No, but it was peaceful.

She went back inside and into the kitchen. Mike had told her to make herself at home. So, she opened cabinets, searching through four of them before she found what she was looking for—a bottle of whiskey. Jim Beam Black. She took a glass and added a couple of ice cubes, then poured a generous amount into it.

Back outside, she sat down in one of the deck chairs, scooting it closer to the railing. She stretched her legs out and took a deep breath of the fresh mountain air. It was quiet and still tonight. No breeze to speak of. She closed her eyes and listened, hearing the river off in the distance. She pictured it, seeing the water splashing across huge boulders as it raced downstream. She let that fade to the background as she stared out into the dark trees. She saw tiny flickers of light and wondered if it was from campfires. Was she that close to the campgrounds?

She took a sip of the whiskey, then leaned her head back. The sky was black dark, and the stars were popping overhead. The air was cool, belying that it was only a few days from June. Or at least what she was used to in June. She supposed up this high in the mountains, it was cool like this all summer. Cool and quiet. In fact, had she ever heard it this quiet before? The moon was low in the western sky, but it was a sliver, more orange than white. Above it was a bright star. A planet, she supposed. Saturn or Venus or something. Sights she'd never noticed in LA.

As she sat there sipping her whiskey, tidbits of her previous life came creeping in, slowly at first, then with a sigh, she let the images come at will. Was she cursed or did she just have bad luck? Or was she—as her captain had told her once—a good cop with a nose for crime? Yeah, at one time, she'd been considered a good cop. That was before she'd killed three people. The last one being the catalyst that moved her from good cop to bad cop.

She knocked back the rest of the whiskey, shoving her thoughts aside before they sent her spiraling into that dark hole of self-loathing. Deep down, she knew she'd done the right thing all three times. Because, yes, she was a good cop. But the last one? Yeah, in the split second that she had—she'd taken the shot. But doing the right thing didn't *make* it right. Far from it. And in the end, it had cost her the job, even though she knew she'd do the same all over again. Because it had been *right*.

Yet here she sat, an FBI agent now, staying at the house of a man she'd met only a few days ago. Why was she still in Timber Falls? Why had she come back at five that morning, just to have coffee with Haley and help her in the kitchen when the breakfast crowd got to be too much for her? Why had she hung around all day, just to meet up with Mike at the saloon for beers and conversation with him and Haley as if they were old friends?

Well, where else should she go? She supposed she could have stayed at the motel for a few more nights. But after spending two days in Timber Falls, the one night in the stark motel room had her feeling lonely and out of sorts. So, she'd headed back up the mountain where at least she knew a couple of people. Bursting in early that morning, seeing Haley's smile as she greeted her, made her glad she'd done it. She didn't feel quite so alone. Even now, sitting out here in the dark, she felt content, not alone. Not really. Peaceful, she thought. And tomorrow morning, bright and early, she'd head down to the saloon for coffee and conversation. And when more people than Haley could handle showed up, she'd go back to the kitchen and crack some eggs.

As she'd told Murdock, she'd hang around until they had something, something to send her off again. Or another murder in another little town that would send her on her way, away from Timber Falls. She'd leave and Mike and Haley would fade from her mind much like any other person she'd met in the last eight months. None of them ever stuck with her, neither names nor faces. Because right now, not a single one came to mind. For some reason, though, she didn't think Haley or Mike would fade away that quickly. She seemed to have made a connection with them.

With a sigh, she stood before loneliness could settle over her. She took one last look out into the darkness, fixing her gaze on a flickering campfire far out in the distance. She paused then, picturing herself at that campfire, a long stick in her hand to stir the flames. There were people sharing the fire with her. There was conversation and light laughter. She was smiling. Happy.

With another sigh, she turned away, noting that no, there wasn't a smile on her face. She wasn't sharing conversation and laughter. She wasn't really happy.

She was alone. Something she thought she should be used to by now.

CHAPTER ELEVEN

Haley glanced to the door, the third or fourth time, keeping a watch out for Carter. It was early. Barely five thirty. She already had the griddle heated, already had the eggs out and bacon ready. She'd unloaded the dishwasher from last night. She had coffee made. She was ready for the breakfast crowd, and she was restless. It was Friday. It would be her last night to sleep in the apartment. Tomorrow would be her last morning to open. CeCe would take over on Sunday morning and hopefully her days could get back to some resemblance of normalcy.

Why, then, was she keeping a watch out for Carter? That certainly wasn't normal. Her only true conversations here were with Mike. With the other regulars, she exchanged only pleasantries and town gossip. Mike was the only one she called a real friend. Yet she found herself waiting for Carter, hoping she'd come again this morning. Maybe it was because Carter was a woman near her own age that she enjoyed chatting with her, enjoyed their conversations. Maybe it was more than that. Maybe it was the gentle teasing, the subtle flirting. Or maybe it wasn't that at all. There was something about Carter, something just below the surface, that intrigued her. Carter was a mystery, wasn't she? Haley knew nothing about her whatsoever, yet Carter had managed to drag out details of Haley's life without much effort.

It didn't matter, though. Carter would be on her way out of town sooner rather than later, off to chase a killer. It was still unsettling to think about a murder in their little town and the locals continued to chat about it at every turn. The tourists? To hear Mike tell it, a few had left the campground early but not many. The other campgrounds were still packed. Everyone seemed to have taken the killing with only a shrug.

She wondered what she would have done had something like that happened back when she and Gail had come here. Would they have left? Yes, she thought that perhaps she would have wanted to. Gail, on the other hand, had always been more adventurous, more fearless. She would have brushed it off as an unfortunate incident—an anomaly—and gone about her business of running the river. And she supposed that's what most of these people were doing.

She saw movement at the door before it opened. Carter stood on the other side, looking at her through the glass. They both seemed to smile at the same time.

"You leave this door unlocked, you never know who might come in."

Haley poured Carter a cup of coffee. "I guess if someone wanted in badly enough, they could just break the glass. Or were you not referring to a killer running loose?"

"I imagine the killer is long gone from here. Thanks," she said, grabbing two sugar packets and dumping them into the coffee.

"Everyone is certainly acting like it. I was just thinking how the killing was met with indifference almost."

Carter nodded. "College students are still young enough that they feel invincible. Something like that always happens to someone else, not them. They probably don't know about the killing in Albuquerque."

Haley added more coffee to her own cup. "How long have you been with the FBI?"

"Eight months."

Haley looked up. "Really? That's all?"

"What? I'm not experienced enough for you?"

"No, I would have assumed longer. I'm only guessing at your age. Midthirties?"

Carter sighed. "Thirty-six. Actually, I guess I'm close enough to thirty-seven to own up to it."

Haley smiled. "How close?"

Carter looked at her watch, presumably to see what date it was. "Less than a week. A few more days to go."

Haley gave a quick laugh. "Yeah, go ahead and count it. It's almost here."

"Says the woman who is only thirty-three." She must have had a quizzical look on her face because Carter added, "Mike told me."

"Why did my age come up?"

"I may have asked. I don't remember."

"Okay. So, you've only been with the FBI eight months. Before that?"

Carter raised her eyebrows. "Why the questions?"

"Because it occurred to me that you asked an awful lot of questions about me, yet I know nothing about you." She didn't miss the shadow that crossed Carter's face or the mask she placed there.

"Nothing exciting. I was a cop in LA. Now I'm with the FBI."

"That's it?"

"That's it."

She leaned her elbows on the bar. "Ever been married?"

Carter met her gaze. "Nope. Never even lived with anyone."

"You're thirty-seven. How did you escape that?"

Carter gave a fake cringe. "Still thirty-six, thank you. And I had a few girlfriends over the years but nothing too serious. The closest would have been Darla. We dated, oh, three years or so."

"Why did you break up?"

"I took a job with the FBI and left. Besides, it wasn't serious either. She dated others besides me."

"Oh. You had an open relationship then?"

Carter smiled at that question. "Is that what you call it? Maybe I should rephrase it—the dating part, I mean. We didn't actually like go out and stuff. Dinner a few times, but not often."

Haley frowned. "Then what?" She leaned back. "Oh. You just…"

"Yeah. We got together at her place a few times a month."

"So she was—"

"Someone I had sex with," Carter said bluntly. "It beat picking up strangers and Darla was willing."

Haley shook her head. "That sounds so…so cold."

"Cold?"

"Emotionless. Or were you friends? Like if you needed someone to talk to, you could call her."

Carter sighed. "I guess I would have called her a friend. We didn't really talk much. In fact, I haven't spoken to her at all since I left LA."

"Wow. I guess you should rephrase. I wouldn't call that dating either."

The bell jingled and she looked away from Carter, seeing the same young couple from the other day. She smiled at them.

"Good morning. Take whatever table you want."

"Good morning. And yes, coffee, please," the woman said before she could offer.

"You staying for breakfast?" she asked Carter as she picked up the coffeepot.

"I can stay for a while. I'm expecting a call from the lab first thing. I'm hoping they'll have something for me."

Haley patted her hand as she walked past. "I wasn't really asking because I expected you to cook. But the company is nice."

And it was. She found Carter easy to talk to. Other than Mike, she couldn't say that about a single other person she'd met in the last seven years. And while she and Mike were friends, he was a man, and the dynamics were different. There were simply some things a guy wouldn't understand as well as another woman.

To that end, she realized how much she missed Gail. Not only as her partner, her spouse, her lover, but as her companion and friend. Someone to talk to.

As she poured coffee, she glanced over at Carter. She was staring into her own cup of coffee, seemingly lost in thought. What a lonely life she must lead. That thought brought back something Carter had said to her when they'd been talking about their normal breakfast fare. She said she made green smoothies before hitting the gym.

"Back when I had a life."

CHAPTER TWELVE

Carter sat out front even though Jewell had told her to take Mike's office. She didn't want to infringe on his space even more than she already was. She'd gotten a text from one of the lab techs while she'd been making a taco for herself in Haley's kitchen. They wanted to do a Zoom call and show her what they'd found. Haley had wrapped up the taco for her and sent her on her way after waving away her offer to pay for breakfast.

"I should be paying you for cooking. Now go!"

She was aware that she was smiling as she set up her laptop on the back table. She liked Haley. She would miss her when she left. She'd probably talked more with Haley in these few short days than she had anyone else in the eight months she'd been on the job. Probably more than anyone in LA the last few years. What the hell did that say about her life?

Her phone dinged and she glanced at it, reading a new text from Zach. *Check your email. I sent the Zoom link.* She nodded and pulled up her email, clicking on the link. Soon, Zach appeared in the familiar box.

"Agent Carter, hello. I'm waiting on Baxter to join us. He can explain the palm prints."

Before she could reply—for she didn't know who Baxter was—another box popped up and a young man appeared. He was smoothing his hair as if primping. He pushed the black glasses more firmly on his nose and smiled into the camera.

"Good morning," he said, almost shyly.

"Good morning," she replied. "I'm Agent Carter."

"Kyle Baxter, ma'am. Nice to meet you."

Zach cleared his throat. "How about you tell her what you found?"

Kyle Baxter's demeanor changed almost immediately, and the shyness left him. "Sure. You want super-duper technical terms or—"

"How about you dummy it down for me," Carter said.

"Good. I prefer that anyway. So, I went over all of the blood smears on the tent—oh, and I'm talking about victim number two, Hayden Anderson here. Anyway, I pieced together the smears. Some were made with fingers only, some had a partial palm print, some made with only the heel of the hand. There was also a partial print found on a rock by the river. We found one good print of the front of the hand which included the index finger." He held up a piece of paper to the camera, showing a handprint. "I printed this out for you, but it's obviously in the file that we'll send you. Anyway, I was able to calculate an approximate size of the killer's hand."

"Okay. How does this help me find him?"

"Oh, yeah. I guess I should have told you this first. Based on the handprint, we can estimate the height too. Now, granted, it's not concrete, but it's based on averages." He held the print up again. "This print is 7.2 inches long. Slightly smaller than the average adult male's hand and slightly larger than the average adult female's hand. So, if we assume it's a male, you're looking at someone around five feet, nine inches, possibly five-ten. For female, about five-seven to eight. And I need to add that since your killer wore gloves, it may have added a fraction or two to the size, but I don't think it would be significant."

She nodded, scribbling down notes even though she knew they'd send her the file later. She knew not to discount possible suspects, but the thought that their killer might be a woman had not crossed her mind. It seemed far too violent for that.

"Strike patterns and blood spatter indicate the killer was right-handed," Zach interjected. "Most of the smear marks were from the right hand, although we found a few that were from a left hand on the outside of the tent."

"Now at the scene of victim number one, Charles Lawson, there were only finger smears, no palm prints at all and even those were partials," Baxter continued. "We collected eight hair fibers, all different. There was nothing under the victim's nails, no evidence that he fought back."

Zach nodded. "And the reason for that—he had flunitrazepam in his system."

She frowned. "Rohypnol? The date-rape drug?"

"Yes. We don't have tox back on Hayden Anderson, but I wouldn't be surprised to find that in his system as well. He, like Charles Lawson, had no defense wounds."

"Okay. What about this book?"

"I used to read that series when I was a kid," Baxter said with a smile. "Loved those books. I wanted to be a park ranger when I grew up. There's always a park ranger that helps the boys out in some way."

She stared into the camera. "Great. But in regard to this case?"

"Oh, yeah. Found no usable prints on either book, although one looked to be well-used while the other appeared to be brand new. We went page by page on the book found in Albuquerque—the older book—and found a few smudges on some pages. They were made by a child and appeared to be grape jelly. That's a guess. It hasn't been analyzed yet."

"So, the killer picked the book up at a used bookstore or, theoretically, he could have already owned the book."

"Might have belonged to his son or even daughter, although the books are marketed to young boys, so we'll assume son." Zach said. "I used to read them too."

"Uh-huh. I've never heard of them before now."

"Well, like I said, it was marketed to young boys."

She looked at her scribbled notes, then back at the camera. "Okay. Anything else?"

"This will be in the ME's report, but vic two was stabbed sixty-four times—fifty of them to his torso—and he had every finger severed except for one." He held a hand up. "Pinky finger on his left hand."

"And his penis was severed and recovered," she said. "Anything I should know about that?"

"It was removed postmortem. Blood and semen were found. Both belonged to the victim. All of the blood samples at both sites belonged to the victims."

"Our first victim was stabbed fifty-four times, right?"

"That's correct," Zach said. "Ten less than Hayden Anderson. And blade lengths, we gave you that info already. And here's something interesting. The ME found the tip of a knife blade imbedded in the sternum of Hayden Anderson. Very small fragment but easy to match if you find the murder weapon."

"Good. That's something. Okay, you'll send me the ME's report and your findings?"

"Doing it now. Final tox report on your victim number two will be in a few days."

She nodded. "Thank you, Zach. And Kyle. I appreciate you not making me drive back down to the lab for this."

"Yes, ma'am, no problem," Zach said. "If you have any questions after you read through the reports, let me know. You have my number."

"Will do. Thanks."

She closed her laptop and blew out a breath. She found Jewell staring at her.

"Stabbed sixty-four times? Someone must have been plenty mad at him."

Carter tilted her head. "You think a woman could have done this?"

"Like a woman scorned?"

"Something like that, yes."

"How did she overpower him?"

"He was drugged. Probably totally out of it."

Before Jewell could answer, Mike walked in. "There you are. Haley said you had a date with the lab guys. Any news?"

"Yeah, got a little. You want to talk?"

He nodded, his two- or three-day stubble full enough to give him a rakish look. "Well, if I'm not nosing into your business, sure, I'd like to go over it with you."

"You growing a beard?"

He rubbed his face. "No. I just hate to shave. Haley says I get quite skanky-looking in the winter."

She followed him into his office, noting the neatly made bed against the far wall. Mike followed her gaze and smiled.

"Yeah, I don't normally leave it quite that tidy. Jewell makes it up for me." He sat down behind his desk and rubbed his hands together. "Okay. Let's go over it."

She sat down too. Yes, Mike was the closest thing she had to a partner. It would be good to run all this by him. And then she'd give Jason all the details and let him do his thing.

And then she'd wait patiently to be told what to do. Hell of a job she had.

CHAPTER THIRTEEN

Haley wiped up the water ring where Butter Bill's mug had been. He'd come in for his usual burger and beer for lunch and had left with a "See you for dinner," tossed over his shoulder. She shook her head with a smile. Yeah, he came in every day but not always for both lunch and dinner. A lifelong bachelor, he moved to Timber Falls after he retired, like a lot of the locals had. Only a handful of them had been born and raised there and even those had moved off at one time or another for work. Bill was seventy-one and well-liked in town. On the occasions he missed dinner at the saloon, he was enjoying a free meal at someone's home. He'd fill her in on it the next day. That was one reason Bill knew most everything that went on in town—he made the rounds and passed on whatever news he'd learned.

Like today. Said it was the craziest thing, but the killing seemed to have brought more people to town, not fewer. Said he'd talked to Sam—of Sam's River Runners—and Sam told him his phone was "ringing off the hook" with people wanting to book runs. Most likely, these folks had never heard of Timber Falls and its Class V rapids until the gruesome murder made the news. Apparently, the chance to run some new, nearly pristine torrents was no match for a possible serial killer.

She looked up as the door opened, automatically smiling as Carter came up to the bar. She was dressed the same as she'd been every single day she'd been there. Black FBI T-shirt, jeans—with a gun and holster clamped on her right side—and hiking boots. And as she usually did, she brushed the hair off her forehead.

"Do you need a haircut?"

Carter raised her eyebrows.

"Because you act like it bothers you," Haley continued.

"I usually keep it shorter, more of a boyish cut." Carter ran a hand through it now. "Other than me taking scissors to it one day for a trim, it's not been cut since I left LA and, yes, it's driving me crazy."

"You should ask Jewell to cut it."

"Jewell? Mike's Jewell?"

"Yes. Although I don't know if you want it that short. She does everything with clippers, not scissors. She cuts Mike's hair every other week."

Carter shook her head. "I'll probably pass on that. Not sure that I want to look like Mike."

Haley laughed. "Did he find you? He came looking earlier."

"Yes. I shared the lab report with him, then we tossed around a few things."

"Like what?"

"Like whether our victims were targeted specifically or if it was a crime of opportunity."

Haley filled a glass with ice, then added tea. "And what did we come up with?"

"We think our killer may have met Charles Lawson—that's the victim in the motel—out on the trail. Followed him or else was invited to the motel. As for Hayden Anderson, our tent victim, that was probably opportunity. His tent was farthest away from the others, close to the river. Charles Lawson was drugged. Hayden Anderson probably too. The question is, how did our killer drug them?"

"Like slipped something in their drink?" She handed her the tea.

"Right. To hear the witnesses tell it, Hayden was up drinking with the group like always. After midnight, they split up and went to bed." Carter took a big swallow. "Thanks."

"You want a burger?"

"I guess."

"Usual?"

"Do I have a usual?"

"Cheeseburger, no tomatoes, extra mustard. Steak fries."

Carter smiled at her. "Oh, so I *am* special. Or do you remember everyone's burger order?"

"As a matter of fact, I do. So no, you're not that special." Then she returned her smile. "Well, maybe a little. You *do* help me in the mornings. And speaking of, tomorrow is my last morning to open. I'm so ready to get back to my house."

"You mean my services aren't needed any longer? Who am I going to chat with then?"

"I'll still be here, only I won't have to come down at five like I normally do. CeCe will handle all the prep work. I can come in about seven, maybe six forty-five. She multitasks much better than I do. If there's a rush at six thirty, she can handle it."

"Okay, so I'll wait to come at seven."

"How long are you going to be in town?"

"I don't know. Gonna miss me when I leave?"

Haley considered the question. "Actually, yes I will. I enjoy your company. As you know, there's no one in town even near my age. Rhonda—who comes in at noon—is in her early fifties. Besides me and Mike, she's the next youngest in town, if that tells you anything."

"Ah. So, it's not necessarily my charming self you're going to miss. It's only the company, huh?"

"The company and, well, cheap labor," she teased. "Can't complain about that part of it."

"I used to work in a little neighborhood diner when I was in high school," Carter supplied. "They didn't let me cook unless someone didn't show up. I mostly bused tables and did the grunt work. But every once in a while, I'd get to do breakfast. I only worked there one summer. It was hell having to be at work at six in the morning."

"I can attest to that. Be right back."

Haley scribbled out Carter's lunch order and took it to Sylvia in the kitchen. On her way back out, she took a pitcher of tea and walked around to the tables, asking if anyone wanted a refill. Rhonda normally did that, but she was busy on the patio as a group of twelve had just sat down. When that order came in, she'd most likely head to the kitchen to help Sylvia. Before she could go back to visit more with Carter, another group came in. Six this time. No, the killing certainly hadn't hampered business. They were as busy as ever.

"Do you have a table open on the patio? We'd really like to sit out by the river."

She shook her head. "Sorry. It's full. But I can push two tables together by the windows. You'll still have a view."

"How long would the wait be for the patio?"

She glanced at her watch. "Maybe a half hour. Or more."

"No, we should probably eat inside. We've got a run at two."

"Right this way then." She led them to the windows, motioning for one of the guys to help her move the tables together. "Taking one of the shorter runs today?"

"We did the long one yesterday. It was awesome. Dead Man flipped us over like that," he said, snapping his fingers. The others laughed.

"Yes, he claims at least one a day, I think."

"We're putting in just past that. Do you run the river?"

She shook her head. "Not in many years. No time." She stood back, letting them sit. "I'll be right out with menus. Tea?"

"I'd rather have a beer," one of the guys said, "but I guess we'll save that for after the river."

She gave a playful wink. "Good choice."

By the time she went back to the bar to retrieve menus, Carter was already eating her burger.

"How is it?"

"Delicious, as always."

Haley patted her arm as she passed by. "You'll be sick of them soon enough."

Between helping Rhonda in the dining room, then helping Sylvia with the lunch orders, she missed Carter. Carter gave a wave through the serving window as she headed out. Haley waved back.

"See you for dinner?"

Carter nodded. "I'll be here."

"She's cute," Sylvia said when Carter had left. "I think she fancies you."

Haley stared at the older woman. In all the years that she'd been in town, no one had ever mentioned her personal life—or lack of. No one had ever asked if she'd been married, if she was dating, if there was someone in another town waiting for her. Not one word. She thought it odd at first, but then realized that the locals really didn't get into each other's business, at least not their personal business. Mike knew about Gail, and she assumed that after all this time, he'd probably passed that on to someone—Jewell, if no one else. Yet no one had ever mentioned a word to her about it. Certainly no one had ever asked if she was gay or even hinted at it. Until now.

"You think so?" she asked casually.

"I've been around long enough to know that look."

"What makes you think I'd be interested in her?"

Sylvia glanced at her a bit shyly. "Word gets around. Besides, I don't think I've ever seen you smile quite this much."

"Smile? I smile all the time," she scoffed.

"Fake smile. You've been doing it for years." She flipped over four hamburger patties without breaking stride. "This is real."

Haley didn't know if she should be offended or not. Were her smiles fake? She might force them sometimes, but she certainly wouldn't call them fake.

"Well, real or not, it doesn't matter, even if I was interested—which I'm not—she'll be leaving soon. In fact, it could be any day, any minute for that matter."

Sylvia took off the meat patties, adding them to the buns that Haley had prepared. "Charlie Wadsworth."

"What about him?"

"His wife died when he was barely thirty. He's spent all this time alone, still grieving. Now he's a bitter, crotchety old man." She looked pointedly at Haley. "You're traveling down that same road, young lady."

Haley didn't know whether she should be angry at Sylvia for speaking to her that way or if she should laugh at the comparison to Charlie, who yes, was a bit on the crusty side. She didn't have time for either, though. She pulled steak fries from the grease—beef tallow, which made them absolutely addicting—then added generous portions to each plate.

She plastered a fake smile on her face as she went to deliver lunch. Yes, she could admit that this one was indeed fake. Because what in the world did she have to smile about?

CHAPTER FOURTEEN

"Do you check in with all your teams this much?" she asked Murdock that afternoon when he called.

"You're the only one I have who works alone and I don't know you well enough to completely trust you yet," he said bluntly. "So where are we?"

"After I met with the lab techs this morning, I called Jason. I gave him everything, emailed him copies of the ME's report. Tox isn't complete on our second victim, but the first one, they found flunitrazepam in his system."

"Really? Rohypnol? I didn't think it had a long shelf life."

"I don't know. Apparently long enough. They found it."

"Okay. So, he was drugged. Couldn't put up a fight. Easy."

"Right. Pizza delivery was at 7:04 and time of death was around two. So between those times, someone came to his door. Rohypnol is most often put into drinks. Did he know his killer? Did he share a drink with him?"

"You have a theory?"

"I think it's a woman. I think he met her out on the trail. Maybe he invites her to his room. She comes in, spikes his drink, kills him."

"A woman?"

"Based on the palm print, it could be either male or female. A little larger than the average female but smaller than the average male."

"Okay. Go on."

"If Hayden Anderson, victim number two, was also drugged, it makes sense. Is he going to let some stranger, a man, into his tent? But a woman? Maybe she comes on to him. He's been drinking, maybe he thinks it's his lucky day. Or night, as it was. Same thing. She spikes his drink. Game over."

"What does Jason think about the woman theory?"

Carter nearly rolled her eyes. Always Jason. While he was nice enough, he normally talked way over her head and made her feel stupid. And she, in turn, tended to be short and abrupt with him. They didn't do idle chitchat, in other words. She only talked to him when necessary—like today. Most of their communication was through email.

"He's going to run the numbers, do some comparisons he said." Whatever the hell that meant, she thought. "He'll let me know as soon as he has something." She looked at the book she'd been holding. "In the meantime, I'm reading a damn children's book. There doesn't appear to be some secret code or hidden evidence in the words. If it's significant, it's for some other reason."

"Okay, Carter. Keep me posted."

She sighed as she recognized the dead silence on the phone. "And goodbye to you. Have a lovely day," she muttered. She leaned back on Mike's sofa and stretched her legs out. "I hate my job and my life sucks." She blew out a breath. Yeah, that pretty much summed it up.

She turned her wrist, looking at the time. It was going on four o'clock. Too early to go to the saloon. That was the lone bright spot in her day, she knew. The Timber Falls Bar and

Grill—the saloon. Yes, she felt right at home there. Well, she'd give it a half hour, at least. With another disinterested sigh, she picked up the book. She flipped it over in her hands a few times, then opened it up, thumbing to the page she'd dog-eared.

CHAPTER FIFTEEN

Haley drew Carter a beer as soon as she saw her walk in. She was early today, she noted. She also noted that the smile she gave Carter wasn't forced or fake. She didn't dwell on that, though. She pointed to a table where Mike sat talking to a woman, a brunette with wavy hair that just touched her shoulders.

"He looks smitten, doesn't he?"

"Who is that?" Carter asked.

"Don't know. She came in about two or so, looking for Mike. I sent her to the station. They came in here about an hour ago." She didn't add that Mike had barely given her a glance. The brunette had his full attention.

"I wouldn't picture her as Mike's type," Carter said before picking up her mug.

"Why is that?"

"Too much makeup, for one. I figured he'd go for someone a little more natural."

"I don't believe he can afford to be choosy. She's been flirting with him. Obnoxiously so."

Carter laughed. "Yeah, I guess I should give him a break. To hear him tell it, it's been a while."

Haley laughed too. "I know." Then she tapped Carter's arm. "They're leaving. Look at him, he's acting like we don't even exist."

But then, at the door, he turned, a huge grin on his face. He gave them an exaggerated wink, then followed the woman out.

"That dog."

"Hope he has fun," Carter said. "Maybe he can share details. It's been a while for all of us, I suppose." She put her mug down. "I mean, I'm just assuming..."

Haley didn't know why, but she blushed. Carter then raised an eyebrow.

"No?"

"I will not discuss sex with you at the bar." She turned away, then paused. "And no, I have not been with anyone but Gail."

Both eyebrows shot up then. "Like...*ever*?"

"Haley...another beer," Scott called from down at the end where he sat next to Charlie.

She ignored Carter's question, moving down to collect Scott's empty mug. "Charlie? You ready for another?"

"Yeah, fill me up."

Was it odd that she'd never slept with anyone but Gail? Maybe to some, but no, she didn't think so. She hadn't even realized she was gay until she went to college. The few guys she dated in high school barely got to first base with her. She wasn't interested and never gave it much thought as to why. Gail wasn't the first lesbian she'd met. No, that was Kelly. Kelly was the one who opened her eyes, but even she only got to second base.

She nearly blushed again, thinking back to those early years. She'd been such a prude, she knew. Poor Kelly had given up finally. Gail was a friend at first, nothing more. But then Gail kissed her unexpectedly and she felt something different than what she'd felt with Kelly. And that first summer, right here in Timber Falls—in a tent—she lost her virginity. And she fell in love. That sweet, sickly young love that made you forget about the world around you. They were inseparable. They were happy and giddy and not worried about a thing. Even graduating college and getting real jobs didn't complicate things much. They settled in Denver—settled into their new jobs and new life. Blake was Gail's coworker who shared a common cubicle wall. He took her on her first long hike, and she was hooked. Their blissful weekends were soon disrupted. Gail was up and gone in the predawn hours on Saturday mornings while she still snuggled under the covers. She—

"Haley?"

She turned, finding Carter staring at her. So were Charlie and Scott. She went back to her task, filling two mugs with beer, pushing those old memories away.

CHAPTER SIXTEEN

She was early. It wasn't even five thirty. Would Haley have the door unlocked already? She parked out front, seeing only a dim light on inside—the kitchen, she supposed. The dining room and bar lights were still off. She walked up to the door anyway. When her hand reached for the doorknob, she hesitated a second, then turned it. It opened as usual, and she went inside, barely registering the jingle of the bell over the door.

Haley was at the bar, the glow from the kitchen light casting a shadow across her face. Their eyes met and she knew that Haley had been waiting for her. A second cup sat on the bar and Haley filled it.

"Good morning," Carter greeted. Her voice was quiet, matching the mood in the bar.

Haley nodded but didn't return her greeting.

"I came a little early," she continued. "We didn't get to visit much last night." Carter tilted her head. "I thought maybe you avoided me on purpose, but you were kinda busy, I guess."

Haley met her gaze again. "Are you lonely, Carter?"

It was an unexpected question, but she answered without hesitation. "Yes. Sometimes more than others."

"Is that why you come here to see me?"

Carter shrugged. "Not really. Or maybe it is. Maybe I just like talking to you." Carter added sugar to her cup. "Are you lonely?"

Haley nodded. "The years kinda got away from me." She twisted the ring on her finger and Carter wondered if she even knew she did that. "I was so devasted when Gail died, I thought surely I would die too. My future seemed lonely and bleak, and I was heartbroken and...well, I was absolutely miserable. And miserable to be around, no doubt. Not that I wanted anyone around."

"You went into a shell?" she guessed.

Haley picked up her cup of coffee then, sipping it slowly as if considering the question carefully. "I suppose you could call it that. My parents tried, they really did, but I wasn't ready then. I was never close to Gail's parents and they were dealing with their own loss. And her hiking buddies—they reached out to me but...well, I didn't want to talk to them."

"You blamed them?"

A deep sigh. "Yes." She met her eyes, holding them. "And worse."

Carter nodded. "Ah. You wished it had been them."

"Yes. How selfish of me, I know."

She didn't say anything. What should she say? Hell, who wouldn't have felt that way? They were quiet for a long moment, both drinking coffee but not speaking. When Haley put her cup down, Carter sensed that Haley wanted to talk. Talk about Gail.

"When I moved up here, I thought I would feel close to Gail, would maybe feel her presence. We spent our summers here during college, we were happy here."

"You fell in love here," she stated, remembering Haley's words.

Haley smiled. "Yes." The smile disappeared as quickly as it had come. "I didn't feel her here, though. Not really. I grieved, I took solitary hikes, I sat for hours and hours in the woods. I had so many memories of her—good memories—yet I never *felt* her. There was only this emptiness."

"But you grieve still?"

"At this point, I don't know if I'm still grieving for Gail or if I'm simply grieving for my lost life, for all the plans we had that were blown away." She added coffee to both their cups. "There are no distractions up here. Especially after the season ends. Long winter months, for sure."

"Lots of time to think?"

"Yes. Lots of alone time. Lots of time to dwell on things."

"And other than Mike, you haven't let anyone get close? You've been alone?"

Haley tucked her hair behind her ears. "Mike and I are friends, but we don't talk about this. And no, I haven't let anyone get close." A quick smile. "There's absolutely no one my age here and certainly no like-minded women."

"No one you left behind? Friends?"

"I didn't have a lot of friends. A small circle. Gail and I were, well, we were selfish with our time together." Haley's face hardened a bit. "I've realized now that she was a bit more selfish with her time, though."

"You mean on her hikes?"

"Yes. During the summers when the weather was favorable, she was gone every Saturday or Sunday—sometimes both." She held her hand up. "Not to say that she didn't invite me along. She did. But I told you, it wasn't my thing. They were so focused on bagging as many fourteeners as possible—that's mountain peaks over fourteen thousand feet—I don't think they even enjoyed the hikes. It was another one to mark off the list, that's all." She held her hand up again. "I sound like I'm complaining, don't I?"

"Complaining? No. To be honest, you sound resentful."

"Oh, that's another selfish word, isn't it? Resentful."

"You think so?"

"Don't you? Yes, I resented it when she'd rather be out on an all-day hike instead of spending time with me. I resented that she couldn't feel happy with a two- or three-hour leisurely hike along a mountain stream. I resented that she wasn't there for breakfast or lunch or even dinner sometimes." Haley closed her eyes, then opened them, meeting her gaze. "Yes, I'm still resentful, but I don't know what for. That she's gone? That my life as I knew it ended that day too? Or still resentful that she put her passion for hiking above me?" Haley looked away from her for a second, then back. "Now I sound bitter, don't I?" she asked quietly.

Carter tried to choose her words carefully. "Outwardly, you say you blame her hiking partners, but inwardly, you seem to blame her. You blame her for your life changing. You blame her for your happiness ending. You blame her for being selfish. And that makes you feel guilty."

Haley stared at her, slowly shaking her head. "I don't feel guilty. Yes, I guess I do blame her but…" She looked away, as if taking assessment of her feelings. "I feel *angry* at her for dying, for leaving me." A deep breath. "And yes, I guess *that* makes me feel guilty," she said very quietly.

"And that guilt makes you feel selfish. It's one big cycle you can't get out of."

"Oh, Carter, you're right. It's like I'm stuck on a damn hamster wheel, and I keep running and running, over and over, and nothing changes." She leaned back against the counter, cup held in her hands. "Nothing changes."

"Are you still working through those stages of grief? What are there? Seven? Five?"

"However many, I've hit them all, I'm sure, even if I keep bouncing back to some of them. Questioning things, you know. The meaning of life and all that." Haley took a sip of her coffee. "Eight years. It'll be eight years on the fifth. Two more days. I always get a little nuts when that date comes around. Sorry you're having to witness it."

"Wow. That's kinda weird."

"How so?"

"That's my birthday."

Haley stared at her for a long moment, then she smiled. "What are the chances that my darkest day is your brightest?"

"Our days are what we make them, Haley. Like you on the hamster wheel…just hop off for once. See what happens."

There was a flash of anger in her eyes. "Don't you think I've tried?"

"Have you? Then why haven't you let someone get close? Why did you push me away?"

Haley's eyes widened. "I haven't pushed you away."

"Sure you have. You said you were unavailable. Said you weren't interested."

"Just because I don't want to have sex with you doesn't mean I've pushed you away. I don't want to have sex with *anyone*, Carter. It's nothing against you."

"Still holding out hope that she'll come back? Maybe her ghost might visit you?"

Haley nearly slammed her cup on the bar. "That was cruel."

She nodded. "Yeah, it was. Sorry." She stood up. "Quit wasting your life, Haley. Gail's not coming back. You wallowing in your resentment and your guilt and whatever else you're piling on is zapping the life from you. And this life is pretty damn short. Quit wasting it."

She turned to go, reaching the door before Haley spoke.

"And what is it that's zapping the life from you, Carter? What is it you haven't told me? What secret do you keep hidden?"

She looked back around, the shadows still veiling Haley's face. She stared at her for a long moment before speaking. "I killed a boy."

She left without another word, going out into the now lightening sky. She paused beside her car, taking in a deep breath of the cool mountain air. She heard the river, heard birds… heard a loud gunshot. It sounded so real, she physically jumped when she heard it.

She looked up into the sky once more, this time seeing images of a crime scene, the blood, the screaming wail of a mother, the slap across her face that felt as fresh as the day she'd received it. Without thinking, she touched her cheek, still feeling the blow.

She turned abruptly then, got in her car, and drove away.

CHAPTER SEVENTEEN

Haley had had a frantic morning and she nearly embraced Sylvia when she came in at ten. A busy Saturday and her last to open—what a great day for her and Carter to have a fight. Oh, it wasn't really a fight. Sure, she'd been angry at her, and she'd tried to hold on to that anger all morning, but in the end, she couldn't. Carter was right on all accounts.

That didn't make serving the breakfast crowd any easier. She'd mixed up orders, burned toast and bacon both, and broken a coffeepot when she hit the corner of the bar. It happened as she'd rushed back after refilling cups and she'd banged it in her haste. Thankfully, it had been all but empty, but the shattered glass had scattered, and she'd only taken the time to sweep it into a pile. She was positively frazzled by the time Sylvia walked in. She didn't realize how much easier it had been with Carter helping her in the kitchen.

Now, as the lunch crowd gathered, she leaned against the back of the bar, sipping tea, watching as Rhonda effortlessly floated between tables, never missing a beat.

"It's because she's not *also* having to cook," she murmured to herself. Of course, she enjoyed being the cook much more than being the waitress. And once CeCe took over, that's exactly what she'd do. Hide away in the kitchen flipping eggs until ten when Sylvia came in.

She looked to the door when it opened, surprised to see Carter. After the way she'd left that morning, she hadn't expected her to come around quite so soon. But there was no friendly smile from her.

"Have you seen Mike?" she asked rather businesslike.

Haley frowned. "As a matter of fact, no, he never came in for breakfast."

"Is that odd?"

"He comes by most mornings, if only to grab coffee."

"I've been driving around all morning. Haven't seen him. I went by the station earlier, but Jewell said she hadn't heard from him all day."

"Have you tried calling him?"

Carter looked at her as if that was a stupid question. "Several times, yes."

"Well, there was the woman he went out with," she reminded Carter. "Maybe he's with her."

"It's almost noon. Does he have that much stamina?"

"You're right." She took her phone out. "Let me try calling him." She frowned as it never rang. "That's odd. It went straight to voicemail. He never turns his phone off." She then called Jewell. It was answered on the second ring.

"Hello, Haley. Are you looking for Mike too?"

"Yes. You haven't seen him?"

"No. Not all day. His Jeep was already gone when I got here this morning. He hasn't called in. I was just packing up to leave too."

"Okay. Well, he's got to be around somewhere. Thanks, Jewell." When she disconnected, she looked at Carter. "I'm kinda getting worried. It's Saturday. He's normally all over the place on Saturdays. If you've been looking, you should have run into him somewhere." Her phone rang and she glanced at it. "Oh, it's Jewell. Maybe she's heard from him."

"Haley, oh my god, send the FBI woman over here. Oh my god," Jewell said again, her voice cracking with emotion.

"What is it?" she asked tersely.

"It's Mike," she said hoarsely. "Mike is here. I went into his office to make his bed up like usual. But...but—"

"Jewell...what's wrong?"

"He's lying in his bed. There's...there's blood, there's... there's a knife."

Haley's eyes flew to Carter's. "We'll be right there, Jewell." She put the phone down, feeling a sense of dread. "She said Mike was in his office, in bed. There was blood." She paused. "And a knife."

"*What?*"

They stared at each other for a second longer, then they both bolted at once, running to the door.

* * *

Carter skidded to a stop in front of the police station. Jewell was at the door waiting for them. Carter could tell her hands were shaking.

"I didn't touch anything," the older woman said. "Well, the doorknob, but—"

"It's okay. Stay here."

Carter went toward Mike's office door, feeling Haley close behind her. The door was standing ajar, and she pushed it open with the knuckles of her hand. She glanced around the room, trying to take it all in. Nothing looked disturbed that she could tell.

She moved closer to the bed, seeing the blood on the pillows, seeing a large knife by Mike's head.

"Oh, Christ," Haley whispered from behind her.

There was a droplet of blood on the beige comforter that covered Mike up to his chest. She took a deep breath, then reached out a hand, touching his neck. His skin was surprisingly warm. There was a pulse.

"He's alive," she said quickly.

"Thank god."

She pulled the sheet off, shocked that there was no blood anywhere on his torso. He simply looked like he was sleeping. She covered his naked body again, then touched his face, noting the warm skin, the even breathing.

"He doesn't appear injured." She glanced at Haley. "Is there a doctor in town?"

"Doctor? No, of course not." Haley grabbed her arm, squeezing. "The knife, Carter. It...it looks like one from the kitchen."

She frowned. "At the saloon?"

"Yes." Haley took a step closer, staring at the knife. "I mean, maybe. It's hard to tell, but the handle, the indentions on the handle are kinda like the ones in the kitchen."

She took her phone out, taking several close-up pictures of the knife, then she stepped back, taking some of the bed. And Mike.

"Okay. Let's see if we can wake him up." She patted his face gently. "Mike? Come on, wake up." She shook his shoulder. "Mike? You in there?"

They heard a groan and she watched as his eyelids fluttered but didn't open.

"Mike! Come on, wake up, buddy," she said again, louder this time.

His eyes finally opened, and he groaned again. "Carter? God, my head hurts."

"Are you injured?" she asked quickly.

He closed his eyes again. "Did somebody shoot me in the head?"

Haley peered around her shoulder. "Mike?"

His eyes opened again. "Haley? What the hell are you doing here?"

"What the hell? We should be asking you what the hell? What happened?"

He tried to sit up but fell back down. "Damn but my head is about to explode."

Carter pulled Haley to her side, speaking quietly. "Try to get him to sit up. I need to call in a forensics team, but I want his story first before they get here."

Haley frowned at her. "What are you saying?"

"I'm saying there's a goddamn bloody knife in his bed, and it doesn't appear to be his blood." She walked away, finding Zach's number, then stopped. "Don't touch anything."

Haley met her gaze, her eyes showing her fear, but she nodded. "Okay. Right."

It rang four, maybe five times before Zach picked up. He sounded rushed.

"Bennett."

"Zach? It's Agent Carter. I need a team. Can you front it?"

"Where are you?"

"Timber Falls."

There was only a slight hesitation. "You got another body up there?"

"Not exactly." She glanced to Mike's bed. "I've got a bloody knife that was left in a bed."

"All right. You need a whole team or what?"

"No."

"Okay. I'll bring Catherine with me. Where?"

"The police station." She paused. "And, Zach, if someone were drugged with Rohypnol, how long does that stay in their system?"

"Are you talking about symptoms of the drug or for a toxicology report?"

"Both, I guess."

"If someone ingests Rohypnol, they can feel the effects of it for about twelve hours or so. Everyone is different. For tox, it'll show up in a blood test for at least twenty-four hours. Urine test, up to fifty hours, sometimes more. Why? You got someone?"

"Maybe. I'll talk to you when you get here."

CHAPTER EIGHTEEN

Mike stared at the knife, then back at Carter. "What the hell is that?"

"You tell me."

Haley paced across Mike's office, hating that Carter was interrogating him like he was a criminal. But yes, where had the knife come from?

"I don't even know what day it is."

Carter ran a hand through her hair. "You're naked. Where are your clothes?"

Mike held his head in both hands. "I don't know, Carter. I don't know."

"Shit, Mike," Carter muttered. She turned to her. "Can you find him some clothes?"

Haley nodded. "Yeah."

Behind Mike's desk was a file cabinet. The two bottom drawers were where he kept his underwear and T-shirts. She didn't pause to wonder how she knew that. His jeans were in a pile on top of an old rolling cart.

"Got forensics coming, Mike. I need to know what happened. Last we saw you, you were heading out with the brunette. Where'd you go?"

Haley turned, watching Mike. His eyes finally showed some signs of comprehension. "Umm, her name was…Sheri, I think." Then he moved his head toward the knife. "Jesus Christ, I didn't kill her, did I?"

"I don't know. Not in here, anyway." Carter moved closer, picking up one of his hands. "You're clean. Makes no sense. Blood on the knife, blood on the pillows. Not a drop on you."

Mike rubbed his eyes. "So, someone planted a goddamn knife?"

Carter squatted down beside the bed. "Who was this woman?"

"I don't know. She…she came in, asking for help with her car." He rubbed his temples with both hands. "She was real flirty." Then he gave a half-smile. "Kinda cute, I guess."

"So where is she?"

He stared at Carter, slowly shaking his head. "I don't know. I don't…remember."

Haley went closer. "You were at the saloon with her. When you left, where did you go?"

"We…I think we…I think we got in my Jeep."

"Right. It's missing," Carter said. "Was she staying in town? Did you go to the motel or lodge? Did you take her to your place?" Then Carter shook her head. "No. I was at your place," she said, as if she'd forgotten where she'd slept last night.

"Everything is fuzzy," Mike said.

Carter blew out a frustrated breath. "Okay. Get dressed. Go with Haley. Get something to eat. I need you to get your shit together."

He frowned at her. "What do you mean?"

She pointed to the knife. "If that knife matches the wounds in our victim, then—"

"Surely to god you don't think Mike had something to do with that." Haley put her hands on her hips. "You're out of your freaking mind."

"No, I don't think he had anything to do with that. But we follow the evidence. Whose prints are on the knife? Hell, whose goddamn blood is it? If Mike's prints are on the knife, then, yeah, he's got some explaining to do." She ran a hand through her hair. "And I should really call the sheriff's department."

Haley pointed at Mike. "He's obviously been drugged."

"I know that." Again, a hand raked through her hair. She turned to Mike. "I want you to give a blood sample when Zach gets here. See what the hell kind of drug you've got in your system."

Mike sat at the edge of the bed and Haley turned away as the sheet slipped off. "Here," she said, handing him some clothes. "Put these on."

He gave a half-smile. "I'm naked and there's two gay women in the room with me. Could be a very cruel joke."

"Come on. Get dressed. We'll go get something to eat."

Carter motioned her out and Haley followed. Jewell was still there, waiting.

"How is he?"

Haley looked at Carter, not knowing if she would be breaking some police protocol by divulging anything to Jewell.

"He's okay," Carter said.

"But the blood, the—"

"Yeah, I've got someone coming for that. Not sure what happened yet."

Haley went to her and patted her arm. "Jewell, why don't you go home. Mike will be fine."

"I've worked for him since the beginning. I know when to keep my mouth shut."

"Look," Carter said. "It appears he's been drugged. I called in the same forensics team that was up here for the killing at the campground. They're going to take the knife, dust for prints, that sort of thing."

Jewell nodded. "And I'll keep that to myself." She looked at Haley. "If you'll let me know how Mike is doing, I'd appreciate that."

"Of course, Jewell."

She turned to Carter when Jewell closed the door. "Mike is like a son to her."

"I'm only forty," Mike said from the doorway of his office. "Let's go with grandson."

"How do you feel?"

"Groggy. But lucid enough to know that my prints better not be on that knife or I'm in a world of trouble."

"I'm more concerned with whose blood it is," Carter said. "If you were knocked out, getting your prints on the knife would have been easy. It's obviously been staged. The blood smears are too neat."

"Where's my Jeep?"

"More importantly, where's this woman?" Carter asked. "Do you have any idea where you went? Hell, did you come here? Did you have her in your bed here?"

Mike shook his head. "I don't remember."

"The bed is too neat," Haley said. "I don't think there was another person in bed with him."

"True. So where could she have been staying? Motel? Lodge?"

"They're normally booked so unless she had prior reservations, I doubt there," Haley said.

"She didn't seem the tent type," Carter said.

"No, she didn't." Haley turned to Mike. "You think her name was Sheri?"

"I think so. Doesn't mean it's her real name."

"I'll ask around," Carter said. "The town's not that big. Surely she couldn't have just disappeared."

CHAPTER NINETEEN

Carter watched from the doorway as Zach measured the knife. He said something to the tech by his side who added something to the iPad she held. Then Zach carefully picked up the knife, leaving a bloody imprint on the once white pillow. She could stand it no more.

"How long is it?"

Zach placed the knife into an evidence bag before responding. "Ten inches."

"Hayden Anderson was killed—"

"With a ten-inch blade," Zach finished for her. "There are a lot of ten-inch blades in the world, Agent Carter." Then he smiled. "But you may be in luck." He brought the knife over. "See the tip?"

She stared at it, an eyebrow raised.

"It's very subtle, but there is an imperfection. Look closely. The very tip is missing," he continued.

"So that could be our murder weapon."

"Correct. We can match it to the strike patterns easily enough, but if this matches the tip that was found in Hayden Anderson's sternum, that would be indisputable." Zach looked back at the bed. "So, the police chief lives here or what?"

"He's a one-man show so he stays here during the summer months when tourists are in town."

"And he has no idea how the knife got here?"

"No. You'll get me the results on his blood test right away?"

"I'll run it as soon as I get back to the lab, yes."

"What about the blood on the knife? I need to know if it's male or female. You can tell that, right?"

"Of course."

"Dare I ask for you to put a rush on this?"

"You and everyone else," Zach murmured as he went back to the bed. "We'll do a preliminary check for fluids—semen, urine and the like. I'm going to take both pillows as well as the sheets and everything."

"Fine." She glanced at her watch. It was nearly two. "I need to head out. Will you lock the door when you leave?"

He looked up then. "If that's the way you want to handle it, sure."

"What does that mean?"

Zach shrugged. "I usually work around crime scene tape."

"Not sure this is the scene of anything. So lock up, will you?"

"Sure thing."

She went outside, wishing she had a partner to work with. Or better yet, a team. How was she supposed to handle all this alone? She should call Murdock, run it by him, she knew. Then she should probably call Jason and fill him in, although how this would help him and his algorithms, she had no clue.

But instead of doing either of those things, she headed to the saloon. Hopefully, Mike would have recovered somewhat. Maybe he remembered something. She also wanted to take a look at Haley's knives.

She found Mike at the bar, sipping on coffee. The place was fairly quiet, and she assumed the lunch crowd had come and gone already. The bar area was entirely empty except for Mike. Haley was nowhere to be seen. She sat down beside him and nudged his arm.

"How are you feeling?"

"Like I've got a damn hangover." He looked at her. "You come to arrest me?"

"Should I?"

"Hell, Carter, I don't remember a thing. Nothing. It's like I blacked out. It's like—"

"Rohypnol."

He nodded. "Yeah. Back in LA, I saw my share of date-rape victims. Some had hazy memories, some had none at all. Some woke up in an alley, naked, signs of sexual trauma—didn't remember a goddamn thing."

"What's the last thing you *do* remember?"

"We left here. In my Jeep, I'm pretty sure." He shook his head. "That's it, that's all I remember." Then he frowned. "No. Wait. She was driving." He closed his eyes. "I remember looking at her, and her face was kinda hazy. Her hands were on the steering wheel, and I remember wondering why the hell she was driving my Jeep."

"You sure it was your Jeep and not her car?"

"I think so, yes."

"That means she would have spiked your drink here in the saloon. She took you directly to the station before you passed out. No way she could have carried you."

"So then what?"

"I don't know. Stripped you, took your clothes. For what reason? To make you think you'd had sex with her." Then she frowned. "*Did* you have sex with her?"

"Hell, I don't know."

"The blood was still fairly fresh." She leaned closer, her voice quiet. "Another thing, not confirmed, but by looks—the tip was missing—it's the same knife that killed Hayden Anderson."

"Oh great. And my prints are going to be on it. I just know it."

"Most likely." She looked around the bar. "Where's Haley? She thought the knife might match the ones they use here."

"Yeah, she told me that. She went upstairs to pack her things and get the room ready, I think."

She nodded. "Oh, yeah. She gets to move home tonight. Speaking of that, I think you should stay at your house too. With me."

"Is it like house arrest? Or are you worried about me? I'm not in any danger, Carter. If someone wanted to kill me—like this woman—they could have done it last night." He rubbed his face. "Why would she do this? Who the hell is she?"

"If the knife matches, then she's our killer."

"Then what the hell did she want with me?"

"I don't know. Maybe you're lucky to be alive, man."

"I could have ended up like that kid in the tent. Christ, I could have had my penis chopped off." He buried his head in his hands. "That'll give me nightmares right there."

"That's what you're worried about? Your penis?"

"I'm worried about—" His phone rang, and he pulled it from his pocket. "Chief Goodson," he answered.

Carter watched as his brows drew together in a frown.

"Last seen when?"

She nearly jumped when a hand touched her shoulder. Haley was behind her.

"Anything new?"

"Yeah, got a few things. You going to your place tonight?"

"I am. And I can't wait to get back into my own bed." She lowered her voice. "How is he?"

"Seems better." She met her gaze. "Do I need to apologize?"

"For what?"

"For this morning."

Haley waved her hand out. "Oh, Carter, no. Everything you said was the truth. Besides, I've already forgotten about it."

"Good. But I am sorry." She motioned to the kitchen. "Can I take a look at your knives?"

"Sure. I already did. I don't think they're the same, or maybe that's wishful thinking. You might want to double check it with your pictures, though."

When she stood up, Mike put a hand on her arm, stopping her as he ended his call. "Not good news, Carter. Not at all."

"Now what?"

"Got a kid missing. Not the same campground as Hayden Anderson. It's the one up the road from that. Trevor something or other is his name. That was Rebecca. She and her husband are the campground hosts up there. He wasn't in his tent this morning, so his friends went on their run without him. They just got back from the river. Still no sign of him."

Carter nodded quickly. "Let's go check it out."

"I should really call the sheriff's department," he said.

"Let me call Zach and see if they're still here. I'll get him to run out with us, take a look at the tent at least. But yeah, give the sheriff's department a call." She paused. "Don't mention the knife."

"You think this is all related?" Haley asked.

"God, I hope not."

CHAPTER TWENTY

As the hour ticked by, Haley found herself walking back and forth behind the bar, her eyes darting to the door at each pass. Was she wrong? Could it really be one of her knives? And if it was, how the hell did someone swipe one? She stopped, her eyes widening. One of her employees? She shook her head. No way. Then how? The back door was left unlocked when they were open. They went out frequently, taking out trash and boxes and such. Again, she shook her head. No. Even if someone were out back, waiting, they couldn't come into the kitchen unseen. There was always someone in there. No. It wasn't one of her knives. It couldn't be.

She glanced down the bar, seeing Charlie watching her. He rubbed his grizzled face, his gray stubble three or four days old now.

"What's got you pacing like a caged tiger?"

She stopped and shook her head. "Nothing."

"No? You're sure fretting about something." He shoved his empty beer mug toward her. "Strange things happening in town, I hear."

She reached for his mug, trying to keep her expression even. "What's that?"

"Heard those crime lab folks were over at the police station. Then heard you drove that FBI gal's car over here to the saloon, with Mike riding shotgun." He scratched his face again. "Then heard one of those lab folks came over here for a bit." He stared at her. "Heard that Mike and that FBI gal took off in her car, not his Jeep. Took off in a hurry, they did. That's what I heard."

She brought him a fresh mug. "You heard all that, huh?"

"Now you're in here, acting all nervous and all." He took a big drink, the foam of the beer catching on his upper lip. He wiped it with the back of his hand. "So what's going on, young Haley?"

She gave him a smile, knowing—as Sylvia had said—it was forced. "I've been sworn to secrecy, Charlie. Sorry."

"Something to do with that kid's murder, no doubt."

Before she could say more, the front door burst open. It was Butter Bill looking as flustered as she'd ever seen him. His face was red, as if he'd jogged over. He nearly fell into his normal barstool at the end, his ample weight making the stool groan when he sat down.

"Beer," he managed between breaths.

"What's got you all in a hurry?" Charlie asked.

"Heard some news."

Haley nearly rolled her eyes as she slid a beer his way. "Not you too."

He took a large swallow, downing nearly half of the mug. "They got a missing camper."

Charlie sat up straighter. "Missing? That's where Mike and the FBI gal ran off to, I reckon."

"Heard it was at the upper campground, below Timber Falls." Bill took another swallow of beer. "Something was going on at the station, too."

"Those lab folks were there," Charlie said. "Haley knows something but she's not sayin'."

She held her hands up. "I don't know anything about a missing camper. I don't know anything at all," she said before going into the kitchen to escape them. God, she wished Mike and Carter would get back.

CHAPTER TWENTY-ONE

"So, is this related to the original killing or not?"

"Hell, Murdock, I don't know. I got a knife. I got a missing camper. Nothing was disturbed in the tent. Nothing at all."

"Why was the knife at the police chief's home?"

Carter leaned against her car, looking through the window into the saloon. Mike was at the bar surrounded by three men. Locals, she knew. She'd seen them there every night. They were grilling him for answers, no doubt.

"Not his home, Murdock. At the station. He sleeps there. He's got a bed there."

"Why?"

"He just does. He's the only cop in town. It's easier that way. But none of that matters. Zach, he's the lab tech who worked the first two scenes, thinks it's the knife used in the second killing. Hayden Anderson."

"So the police chief is a suspect?"

"No, he's not a suspect."

"Then what the hell is going on?"

She could hear the frustration in his voice, and she tried not to match it. "He was drugged. They took a blood test. Zach is going to let me know the results tomorrow, hopefully."

"Is the sheriff's department involved?"

"Chief Goodson called them. They're involved only in the missing camper. I didn't mention the knife to them. They came up, took some statements at the campground, looked around a bit. There was no sign of a struggle. No sign he'd slept in the tent the night before. If he doesn't show up by morning, I think the plan is to call in a search and rescue team and start looking for the guy. That's what I heard from one of the deputies anyway." She blew out a breath. "There was a woman. She's a person of interest. Only I don't know her name. She was with Mike—the police chief. I think she drugged him, left the knife, took his Jeep. The Jeep is his official police vehicle."

"You think, Carter? What evidence do you have?"

"None."

"How do you know Goodson is not involved? If his prints are on the knife—"

"Oh, hell, Murdock, he's not involved. I told you, he was drugged. He—"

"Carter, if his prints are on the murder weapon, then you've got to consider that he's involved. You need to let the sheriff's department know about—"

"No, Murdock. Look, I know I haven't been with you long, but I know what the hell I'm doing. I know how to read people and I know when someone is not telling me the truth." She ran her fingers through her hair. "Yes, his prints will most likely be on the knife. I know we have to consider that, but my gut tells me this is all staged."

"Blood on the knife?"

"I don't expect anything until tomorrow. They'll run it, of course."

"I'm sure you've considered this, but you've got a woman missing. A woman who was last seen with your police chief. If the blood is female, then—"

"I know, Murdock."

"If he was drugged, he could have killed this woman and not remembered."

"If he was drugged with Rohypnol, he wouldn't have been capable of killing someone. But let's don't forget, he was found in his bed, naked, passed out. There were no clothes found, no vehicle. I doubt he stashed his Jeep somewhere, hid his clothes, walked naked through town to the station, drugged himself, then crawled into bed."

"So you have considered it? Good. Since you've been staying there in Timber Falls, I was afraid you'd befriended this guy and it was clouding your judgment. Like maybe you were covering for a friend."

She glanced again to the window, seeing familiar faces. Friends, yes. Mike and Haley were her friends. She looked up into the darkening sky, watching as the first stars of evening showed themselves.

"No, Murdock. I have no friends. My judgment is sound. You can trust me on this."

"Okay, Carter. Have you been in touch with Jason yet?"

"No. I'll call him in the morning."

"Good. Keep me informed. I'll be in touch with the sheriff's department there. If this missing camper turns up dead, we'll take the lead on it, not them. If you need help, I can send in a team. Reynolds is in Las Vegas. They've about wrapped it up there. I could—"

"I'm fine for now. Thanks."

"Okay. Your call, Carter." He paused. "For now."

She pocketed her phone. She had nothing against Reynolds other than his penchant for sticking rigidly to the book. She feared if Reynolds was here, Mike would most likely be in his own jail tomorrow when the lab reports came back. Of course, Timber Falls didn't have a jail. No, Reynolds would have him cuffed and headed down the mountain to the county jail where he'd be stuck until she could find something to clear him.

With a sigh, she glanced into the saloon, seeing Haley looking out the window. Looking for her, maybe?

CHAPTER TWENTY-TWO

"Are you on duty or can you have a beer?" Haley asked as Carter sat down beside Mike. Mike hadn't wanted a beer. He was drinking water.

"Beer, please. It's been one of those days."

Haley glanced down the bar to where the guys—Scott, Charlie, and Butter Bill—were and nodded. Oh, yeah. One of those days. They hadn't stopped talking. Arguing among themselves, really.

She placed the mug near her, then leaned closer, her voice quiet. "Everything okay?"

Carter seemed to know what she meant. "So far, at least. Lab results will dictate the course."

"You know my prints will be on the damn knife," Mike said, his voice as quiet as hers.

"Most likely," Carter agreed. "We'll deal with it then."

Mike turned to Carter. "I didn't kill anyone."

"No. It'll all work out."

"Will it?"

Carter took a drink of her beer. "You'll sleep in your own bed tonight. I'll be there too. We'll start fresh in the morning."

"This missing camper," Mike continued. "I heard they're going to bring in a SAR team at first light. Going to search along the hiking trails that leave from the campground and in the immediate area. The guy's car was still there. Locked."

"Maybe he fell in the river and drowned," Haley offered.

"That's always a consideration, but his body would have been spotted by now, as many rafts that are on the river," Mike said.

"Scott heard the missing camper was just nineteen," she said. "Is that true?"

"I don't know," Carter said. "But I don't think we're going to find him alive." She leaned closer to Mike, keeping her voice low. "I think this woman is the killer. I think she killed this guy, hid him somewhere, and then left the knife with you. I think the blood on the knife will come back male."

"You just guessing, or you know something?"

She gave a slight shrug. "Guessing."

"If this woman is the killer," Haley whispered, "why him?" she asked, pointing to Mike.

"Serial killers are hard to figure out," she said. "None are alike…yet they're all alike. They may have different reasons for killing or a different trigger, but at the end of the day, they're all driven by a compulsion to kill."

"I'm still alive."

Carter turned to Mike. "Why is that I wonder? What game is being played?"

"She's trying to frame me for something."

"But for what?"

"Hell, I don't know, Carter. Maybe it's random. Maybe I'm the unlucky guy she picked to fuck with."

"I'm not a detective or anything," Haley said, "but if you're targeting someone at random to fuck with, as you say, are you really going to pick a cop?"

"No, you're not." Carter took a drink of her beer. "There has to be a reason."

Haley leaned closer to Mike. "Who have you pissed off?" she asked quietly.

"Even if I pissed someone off, are they really going to kill people to get back at me? I mean, that's assuming she killed the guy in the tent."

"The knife matches," she reminded him.

Mike jerked his head around. "It's been confirmed?"

She shook her head. "Just visual, per Zach, it looks like the same knife. The tip was missing. Doubt it's a coincidence."

Mike let out a weary sigh. "And my prints will be on it."

"Like I said, we'll deal with it tomorrow."

"Easy for you to say. I—"

"Won't do any good to worry about it. You'll go home with me. We'll have a shot of whiskey and go to bed."

"You found my whiskey?"

"Of course," she said, tipping her almost empty mug at him. Then she glanced at Haley. "What about you? You working the late shift?"

"Yes. Saturdays are busy. But I get to go home tonight and sleep in." She looked at Scott, who held up three fingers. "If you call six sleeping in, that is."

Carter nudged Mike. "I feel like a steak tonight. Let me buy you one."

"I don't have much of an appetite. Getting framed for murder will do that."

"Mike, it was so obviously staged, a rookie cop could see that. We'll start fresh tomorrow, early."

Haley filled three mugs for the guys, all the while keeping an eye on Mike. His brow was etched with worry.

"Wonder where the hell she took my Jeep? Did you report that?"

"No. We'll deal with that tomorrow too."

Haley sighed, then moved down the bar to deliver the three frosty mugs. When she came back, Carter got her attention.

"Can I take a look at your knives now? Not that it'll make much difference, but I'd like to know one way or the other. If they do match, it'll be just another piece of the puzzle of trying to frame Mike."

"Of course. Come on back."

She walked around the bar and followed Haley into the kitchen. She pulled up the pictures on her phone while Haley went to find her a knife. It was close. Very close. "Not the same pattern. Close." She held the phone up for Haley to see.

Haley let out a relieved breath. "Good. I've been worried all day, wondering how the killer could have gotten into the kitchen. Glad to know he didn't." She paused. "Or she."

* * *

She and Mike leaned on the deck railing, looking out into the darkness, both holding a tumbler of whiskey. Mike had barely touched his.

"Are those campfires?"

"Yeah. That's from the upper campground." He turned to face her. "I got a bad feeling about all of this, Carter."

"No doubt. But we can only deal with what we've got."

"If my prints are on the knife, the sheriff's department is going to want some answers. Hell, I know all those guys, but still, how the hell—"

"Mike, you were drugged. That's how your prints got on the knife."

"It looks like—"

"What? You passed out and conveniently left the knife there so that you'd be implicated in a murder? It was staged. I took pictures. Zach took pictures. So will you quit worrying?"

"I'm not going to sleep a wink tonight."

She returned her gaze to the trees, staring at but not really seeing the twinkling campfires. "Tell me more about Haley."

"What about her?" Mike took a sip of his whiskey. "You got a thing for her or what?"

"A thing?"

"You're over there helping her cook every morning."

"Doesn't mean I have a *thing*." She set her glass down on the railing. "She's lonely, I'm lonely. We talk. That's all."

"You're lonely?"

She smiled. "I have no home and no friends. So yeah, I'm lonely."

"I take it you're not loving the job then?"

"Not really. And if I'm being truthful, I wasn't really loving the job back in LA either."

"It's easy to get burned out on it. I should know." He shifted beside her. "You see so much shit, man. It takes its toll. One time, we got called in to a scene where the stepfather had raped the two daughters. The mother was stoned out of her mind, the stepfather was high on god knows what, and those two little girls were all bloody and crying. Hell, one of them was only ten years old. Their little brother, who was eight, called 911. How do you make goddamn sense of that?"

"You can't."

"No, you can't. And that bastard ruined three lives. Those little girls will never be the same. And the boy? He watched it all. What the hell is that going to do to him?"

"Was that your last case?"

"I wish. No, I stuck it out for another year. My wife stuck it out for another year, I should say. Can't blame her for leaving me. She wanted to have kids, a family. She told me I'd make a lousy father. I wasn't home enough, and I wasn't compassionate enough." Mike looked at her. "I'll give her the first one, but compassionate? Hell, I took that job to heart. I was *too* compassionate."

"The good ones are."

"Yeah. That's why the good ones don't last." He knocked back the rest of his whiskey. "That's why we get burnout, Carter. We care too much. It eats at you after a while." He nudged her arm with his elbow. "I'll be your friend, Carter. And I'd be happy to call you one."

She laughed quietly. "I guess so. You're counting on me to keep your ass out of jail."

CHAPTER TWENTY-THREE

Carter stumbled over a rock and Haley reached out a hand to steady her. They were on a steep trail up near the falls—Timber Falls. Haley, like a host of other locals and guests, had volunteered to help search for Trevor Greene, age nineteen. The SAR team had gathered everyone near the campground, separating them out into teams and dispersing them along the nearby trails. The SAR team itself would be bushwhacking between the trails on horseback. Mike and Scott, one of the locals she'd met at the bar, were on her team. They were some sixty or seventy yards ahead of them.

"Thanks. Hiking is harder than it looks."

"Are you winded?"

"Do I sound like it?"

Haley gave a quick laugh. "A little, yes. But you've been up here nearly a week. I imagine you've acclimated to the altitude some by now."

"I used to keep in shape, go to the gym. Since I've been on this job, that's stopped. And I know it's an excuse. I could take a run each morning if I wanted."

"But?" Haley prompted.

"Haven't really felt like it, I guess."

Haley stopped walking and she did too.

"You want to tell me about it?"

"About?"

"About the boy you killed. Or is it something you don't talk about?"

She looked up ahead to where Mike and Scott were. They had stopped too. Mike turned back around and gave them a wave. Carter lifted her hand to return it.

"I talked to a shrink. That's standard practice." She turned to look at Haley. "It was a clean shoot. Justified. But I was made out to be the villain."

"Tell me."

She took a deep breath, then started walking again. "I was at a convenience store, getting gas. I happened to turn and glance inside through the window. I saw what appeared to be an armed robbery in progress." She stopped again, seeing it all in her mind. "I didn't call it in. I went right up to the door, went inside. The kid turned, pointed his gun at me, I fired." She kicked at a rock, seeing the boy lying there on the dirty floor. Then she heard the frantic screams from outside. She was pushed away as the boy's mother knelt at his side.

"What else?"

She took a deep breath. "It was a toy gun. The kid was only fourteen. Good kid. Straight A student. His father was ill. They didn't have insurance. He was trying to get money for his dad's medications."

"Oh, Carter."

"Yeah, pretty much sucked. The media raked me over the coals for sure. My picture was in the paper nearly every day while they ran stories about the kid and his family." She started walking again. "And then they started digging into my past. I'd been on the force fifteen years. This was my third shooting." She glanced at Haley. "All dead."

"So does that make you a good cop or a bad cop?"

She smiled at that. "The first two, I was a good cop. Saved a woman's life, got a medal. The other was a gang banger, wanted for six murders. Got another medal." She shrugged. "Apparently, I was trigger happy. Apparently, I liked killing people."

"But you couldn't have known it was a toy gun."

"No. It looked real enough. The clerk thought so too. The whole thing was on the security cameras. I did everything right. Didn't matter. They wanted me gone. Everyone wanted me gone. No one wanted to work with me."

"What were you supposed to do? Let the kid shoot you?"

"There's only a split second to process it all. Yet in that split second, I knew he was just a scared kid. In that brief moment, I could see the fear in his eyes." She stopped, staring up into the sky. God, she'd gone over and over and over it in her mind. So many different ways it could have ended. But it didn't. "Just a split second and he was dead," she said quietly.

"So even though you did everything right, you blame yourself for his death?"

"Of course. Isn't that what we do?" She glanced at her. "I mean as humans. As good, decent people, isn't that what we do?"

"So you blamed you, the media blamed you, everyone blamed you."

"Yeah. And it wouldn't go away. Every day there was something in the paper about it. Human interest story and all. Kid is trying to do good and help his family. Mean old cop comes along and kills him."

"That's ridiculous."

"That was the narrative."

"There are other ways to help your family. How about a GoFundMe page or something?" Haley touched her arm. "I'm sorry. I sure this still affects you terribly."

"I don't think about it as much as I used to. It's been ten months." She laughed lightly. "Oh, that's a lie. It crosses my mind almost every day. I don't have dreams about it anymore, though. Not much."

"So you lived with it for two months before the FBI?"

"Yes. And by that time, I was ready to leave too. If this hadn't come up, I would have quit. The stress was enormous, and I wasn't handling it very well. It was time for me to go."

"Had you always wanted to be a cop?"

She nodded. "I watched too much TV as a kid. It was all I ever wanted to do."

"What about your family?"

She shook her head. "I'm the middle child. The forgotten middle child, I like to say."

"What does that mean?"

"That means that Reggie—my handsome older brother—and Laurel—the pretty young princess—were the darlings in the family. I was just there, in the way."

"Troubled teen or anything?"

"Me?" Carter smiled and shook her head. "I was a good kid. Studious. Didn't get into trouble at all. Can't say the same about them."

"Yet your parents fancied them over you?"

"Always. I learned that I was an unplanned pregnancy, and they weren't ready for another kid. My brother is only fifteen months older than me. They catered to him, and he learned at an early age that he could get away with murder. I was five when Laurel came around. She was cute and charming, and they called her Princess."

"Oh, god, that's nauseating."

Carter laughed. "Yeah, it was."

"I take it you're not close?"

"Oh, we're civil when we talk, which is seldom. She's married, got a couple of kids, lives in the suburbs. Reggie has been married and divorced three times. He's currently living with my parents."

"Do you keep in touch with them?"

"Only when my mother calls. She reminds me how adorable Laurel's kids are and how poor Reggie has had a rough go of it." She paused. "She never asks how I'm doing."

"What about after the shooting?"

"She said it was an embarrassment to see my picture in the paper."

"Good lord, is she a cold bitch or what?"

Carter laughed out loud. "You've never met the woman, yet you've described her perfectly."

"I'm sorry, Carter. A parent should never—"

"It's okay. I'm way past the point of worrying over it. There's no real relationship with them. I've accepted that as fact. I accepted that a long time ago. And to be honest, it's quite freeing. I don't rely on them for anything, therefore I don't owe them anything."

"Did you even tell them you left town?"

"No. When this came up, I had about three days to get everything in order before I was on a plane to Phoenix." She stopped suddenly, seeing a reflection through the trees. "Look there. What is that?"

Haley followed her gaze. "Looks like a car windshield or something."

She looked up to where Mike and Scott were ahead of them. "Hey, Mike," she called. "Come back down. I need the binoculars." She stared into the trees where the reflection was. "How the hell could a vehicle have gotten there? Certainly not on this trail."

"No. There's a short forest road—Creek Road—on the back side of this little canyon. It'll take you up to Cinnamon Creek. It dead-ends up there."

"Where the locals fish," she murmured.

"Right."

"Maybe someone is parked there then."

"No, the creek access is much farther back."

"What's up?" Mike asked when he came sliding back down the trail. "See something?"

She pointed into the trees. "A reflection or something."

Mike held the binoculars to his face. "Son of a bitch. That's my goddamn Jeep." He handed them to her. "It must be off of Creek Road."

She turned the focus wheel, seeing the dark shape of the Jeep hidden in the trees. "Can we hike to it from here?" she asked no one in particular.

"I think so," Haley said. "It'll be steep and rocky, but we should be able to make it."

"Hell of a lot shorter than going back down to the road," Scott offered.

"Then let's go."

CHAPTER TWENTY-FOUR

Carter was nearly gasping for breath by the time they'd slipped and stumbled their way to the bottom of the canyon and then climbed back up the other side. Haley had teased her, saying it was barely steep enough to even call it a canyon. Regardless, she clung to a tree at the top.

"You don't look like you should be out of shape," Scott said.

"Hell, she came from damn near sea level," Mike said. "Give her a break."

"Thank you," she managed between breaths.

"But yeah, I'd have thought you'd be a little fitter," he added, drawing a laugh from Haley.

"I think you're doing great, Lynn."

"Lynn?" Scott asked. "That your name?"

"You can call me Carter. Shall we push on?"

Silly question since it was her that they were all waiting on. She let Mike take the lead, hoping he'd go a little slower than the near sprint Haley had had them on earlier. It didn't matter, though. The terrain leveled out and it was fairly easy going.

Looking at the Jeep through binoculars had made it seem a lot closer than it actually was. She glanced at her watch now. It had taken them more than forty-five minutes to cross the canyon.

"It's not really hidden," Mike said. "It's right off the road."

"Wanted to make sure it was found," she said.

Mike opened the driver's door, then stepped back. "Got blood." He met her eyes. "Shit, I hope—"

"There's a body in the back," Haley said, her voice shaky.

Carter moved Mike out of the way, then opened the back door. It was a bloody mess. She stared at the body, seeing the young man's face nearly covered in blood.

"Son of a bitch," Mike murmured beside her. "He was killed right here in my goddamn Jeep."

"Holy shit," Scott mumbled from behind them. "Is that the guy?"

Carter closed the door, blocking their view of the body.

"Let me call it in."

CHAPTER TWENTY-FIVE

"You've got to calm down," Haley told him. "No one thinks you killed him."

"Don't they? Hell, maybe I did. I can't remember a goddamn thing!"

She grasped his arms. "Stop it. You know good and well you did not kill anybody. And lower your voice." She pointed to the Jeep where Carter was talking to the three sheriff's deputies who had driven up. "Besides, she will not let anything happen to you."

"They don't even know about the knife yet. Wait until that bit of news gets out." He ran a hand through his short hair. "Damn, Haley, this not knowing, not being able to remember, it's driving me crazy."

"I imagine it is. But you've got to hold it together." Then she frowned. "Shouldn't you be over there with them?"

"Well, you know, other than it's not my jurisdiction outside of the so-called 'city limits,'" he said, making quotations in the air, "my Jeep has a goddamn body in it. Kinda a conflict of interest, don't you think?"

She arched an eyebrow. "Carter told you to hang back?"

He sighed. "Yeah."

Haley heard another vehicle approach and she turned, seeing a white van pull up. The same man from yesterday got out—Zach. He had three others with him. She heard what she assumed was a greeting exchanged between him and Carter, but she couldn't make out the words. Another man walking beside him nodded at something Carter said, then he shoved his black glasses a little higher on his nose before opening the back door of the Jeep.

She turned away from the sight. She had only glanced inside when they'd opened the door earlier, but that was enough as she thought she might very well lose her breakfast. The others had seemed unaffected by it—the body, the blood—and she supposed it was something they were used to. She, however, was not. Scott, too, hadn't wanted to hang around. He'd caught a ride back to town and if not for the panicked look on Mike's face, she would have joined him. Scott was already, no doubt, sitting on a barstool sharing his experience with Charlie and Butter Bill by now.

Carter's cell rang and she stepped away from the Jeep, moving back toward the road as she spoke. The deputies stood off to the side, watching as Zach and his crew went to work.

"Who do you think she's talking to?"

Mike shrugged. "Maybe her commander."

"She didn't mention it to me, but did she get the lab results she was waiting on?"

"I doubt it. We were out on the trails at dawn. Maybe that's the lab then." He ran a nervous hand through his hair once more. "My prints will be on the knife. There's a goddamn body in my Jeep! I'm so screwed."

"Jesus Christ, Mike! Lower your voice," she nearly hissed at him and pulled him farther away from the deputies. "Okay, so she's off the phone and now she's talking to the deputies again," she nearly whispered.

"She probably got lab results. They're going over the best way to arrest me. Maybe they think I'll make a run for it." He turned around, looking into the woods. "Maybe I should."

Haley rolled her eyes. "Will you stop?"

"Will you come visit me in prison?"

She smiled and touched his cheek affectionately. "Yes, I will. Once a week."

He smiled too. "And bring me cookies?"

"Don't push your luck." She squeezed his arm. "Okay, something's happening. One of the deputies is on the phone now, and he's motioning to the others. Carter is looking at us. Okay, no, she looked away again."

Mike slowly glanced over his shoulder, looking out of the corner of his eye. "Looks like they're leaving."

"Hey, Mike," one of the deputies called. "Call us if you need help with anything."

"What the hell does that mean?" he murmured under his breath, then lifted a hand at them. "Thanks, Harmon. See you later."

"They just left? That's kinda anticlimactic, isn't it?"

Mike let out such a relieved breath, his shoulders sagged. "Better than having them arrest me. I have a reprieve, it looks like."

Carter came over then, a smile on her face. "That went better than I expected."

"I'll say." He held his hands up. "I'm not in cuffs."

"And you won't be. It's our case, not theirs. Well, I mean *my* case, but I'll need your help."

"The FBI is taking over?"

"Yes. Hunting for a serial killer is more my thing than theirs. I should clarify—mine and Jason."

"Who is Jason?" Haley asked.

"The computer whiz at Quantico that I use. Or maybe I should say he uses me. Regardless, Murdock—he's my boss—says it's mine."

"So they're out of the loop?" Mike asked.

"Unless I need them for backup or something. Even then, they're an hour away. I told Murdock you and I could handle it."

"I take it he doesn't know about the knife?"

"He does." Carter clapped his shoulder. "I told him you weren't the killer. He's going to trust me on it. For now. I think he's got a team on standby."

"A team?" Haley asked.

"Reynolds's team. They're the ones I trained with." Carter motioned back to the Jeep. "I'm going to stay until they're finished. Catch a ride back down with them. Why don't you call Jewell or somebody and get them to pick you up?"

"I can stay too," Mike offered. "I mean…"

Carter looked at him for a long moment, then nodded. "Okay. I guess it'll save me having to fill you in later." Carter turned to her. "Can you get a ride?"

"Yes, I'll ask Rhonda to drive up. No problem." She and Mike started to walk off, but Haley touched Carter's arm to stop her. "You'll come by the saloon later?"

"Of course. It'll be a while, though. We'll have to stay up here until the ME comes to collect the body."

"Okay, sure. I understand. I'll see you later then."

Carter held her gaze and Haley saw the questions there. But Carter said nothing more before turning and going back to the Jeep.

Haley found herself twisting her wedding band as she watched her walk away.

CHAPTER TWENTY-SIX

Carter tried not to hover behind Zach and Baxter as they worked, but she found herself peering over their shoulders more often than not.

"Something you're looking for, Agent Carter?" Zach asked without turning around.

"How about some brunette hairs, shoulder length?"

Zach turned then and smiled. "Got some of those, yes."

"Really? In the back seat?"

"Yep."

She let out a breath. "Great."

"Great?"

"That means the woman—and not Mike—was back there with our victim." She looked at Mike. "That's good news."

Zach stopped then and came out of the Jeep. "About that. The prints on the knife…"

"Were mine?" Mike asked.

"Yes. But they were almost too perfect. Staged, as Agent Carter here predicted."

"Was he drugged?"

"Oh, yes. I meant to call you first thing this morning, but it got away from me." He pointed to the Jeep. "And now this. But yes, flunitrazepam. Same as both victims."

"Both? You got tox back on Hayden Anderson?"

"Yes. Did you not get it? I emailed it to both you and the deputies working the case. But I overheard earlier—they're no longer involved?"

"This looks to be victim number three of a serial killer, so I'm taking the lead. But I've been up here since daybreak. I haven't checked email."

"Both of their tox reports were surprisingly similar." He shrugged. "Or not surprisingly considering it's the same killer." He went back to the Jeep. "Taking a guess at stab wounds here— over forty. Unlike Hayden Anderson, though, only three fingers were severed." He held one up to show them. "While forty stab wounds may seem violent, this scene doesn't appear to be nearly as furious as the last one. Blood spatter is consistent with the stab wounds only."

She nodded. "The tent, a lot of that was intentionally smeared."

"Correct. This scene looks like the killer did their business and left. Which is odd, considering how remote this is."

"Remote, meaning plenty of time to cut off many more body parts?" Mike asked.

"Precisely."

"Maybe that's the reason," she said. "All the blood and gore at the tent was for show. Up here? Who's going to see it? A deer? A bear? Why bother with a scene."

Zach laughed lightly but said nothing as he stuck his head back inside the Jeep. She and Mike took a step away, letting them work.

A few minutes later, Baxter held up the victim's right hand. "Got blood under his nails. Could be a defense wound."

"Could be his own blood," Zach countered.

"Only one way to find out."

"Hey! Look here," Zach said, holding up a familiar book. "If there was any doubt you had a serial killer, this should do it."

Mike nudged her. "Wanna bet my prints are on that book?"

CHAPTER TWENTY-SEVEN

"It's got to be something from your past." Carter sat down next to him, their chairs pulled into the shade of the corner pine that grew close to the deck.

"Hell, I've been gone from LA ten years. It can't be that."

"Someone is trying to frame you for murder. It's not random, Mike."

"You really think this woman did that? All three murders?"

"What? You think maybe someone put her up to it? To spike your drink, I mean."

"Could be."

Sure, there could be another party involved. But it still came back to Mike. It had been after one when they'd finished with Zach and his team, and the body had been removed. They'd stopped off at the saloon for a late lunch, but Haley had already gone for the day. Mike said she normally cut out at noon on Sundays. After burgers, they'd come back here to Mike's place. He to make arrangements to get his Jeep towed to the lab—Zach's request—and she to compose a lengthy email to Jason, including the lab reports. Being Sunday, she hadn't expected to hear from him, but he'd called her, and they'd talked for nearly an hour, far longer than her normal conversations with him. He agreed that they should be looking for someone from Mike's past. That meant digging into LAPD's records which he said would take him a day or two. He also echoed Murdock's words—was she *sure* Mike Goodson wasn't involved?

Mike sighed heavily, then stood. "Man, I don't guess I've recovered yet. I feel wiped out." He pointed to the house. "Gonna head to bed."

She raised her eyebrows. It was still at least an hour from sunset. "Gonna take a nap?"

"Gonna shower and get into bed and sleep until morning. Hopefully."

She nodded. "Okay. So if I wanted to go visit Haley, where do I go?"

Mike grinned at her. "Yeah, I think you do have a thing for her." He moved over to the railing. "Come here. You can just see the roof of her house. Take you about ten minutes to walk over. There's a trail."

* * *

She did just that, the walk taking her twelve minutes, not ten. She stood by the front door, about to knock, when she decided to go around to the deck. Like Mike's house, Haley's was on a slope too, the deck facing west and the sunset. She walked around the cabin, her boots crunching on pine needles as she went. She paused at the bottom of the steps—six or eight of them—then walked silently up to the deck.

Haley was sitting in a chair which had been pulled out into the waning sunlight. Its matching partner was still against the wall of the house.

"Hey."

Haley jerked her head around, then quickly looked away, her hands brushing at her cheeks. She stood then and went to the railing, keeping her back to her.

"Hey, Carter. What are you doing here?"

Carter went over to her, touching her arm to turn her around. Haley's tearstained eyes met hers. "You don't have to hide your tears from me."

They stared at each other for a long moment, then Haley finally nodded. "No, I don't suppose I do."

Carter nodded too, then went to get the second chair and placed it next to Haley's. She sat down and Haley did the same.

"Mike said you usually leave the saloon at noon on Sundays."

"Yes, I need some downtime and Sundays are the best."

"Yeah, Mike said it's your open window. Half of last week's tourists have left, and the next group haven't come yet."

"Yes, the lull between shifts the locals call it. I imagine when news gets out about our latest casualty, there may be more of a lull than normal."

"You think so?"

Haley shrugged. "Hard to know what college students will do. The first killing hardly caused a stir. Two? If it were me, I wouldn't come anywhere near Timber Falls."

"Yeah, some guy from the forest service called Mike, letting him know they were thinking about closing the campgrounds."

"I expected that. The RV park is privately owned, though. I wouldn't think they would close. Again, if it was me staying there, I'd—"

"Get the hell out?"

Haley gave a short laugh. "Yes." She glanced over at her. "You want something to drink?"

"What do you have?"

"I have a few bottles of wine. There's some whiskey that Mike keeps here. No beer."

"No?"

"I serve that enough at the saloon. I can barely stand to look at it."

"Don't drink it?"

"If I'm at Mike's, I'll have a beer with him. Speaking of him, where is he?"

"He went to bed. Said he hadn't recovered yet."

"I'm sure the stress is getting to him. He was totally freaking out earlier."

"Yeah, I know. It'll all work out."

Haley stood up. "A drink?"

Carter nodded. "Okay, sure. I'll have whatever you're having."

Haley smiled at her. "I didn't picture you as a wine drinker."

"I can tolerate it."

"So? One ice cube or two for your whiskey?"

Carter laughed. "Two, please."

Her gaze followed Haley inside, then her smile faded. Haley had been crying. Was that a usual occurrence on her Sunday afternoons alone? Or was it because tomorrow was the anniversary of Gail's death? She gave a quick, humorless laugh. And her own thirty-seventh birthday. Where had the years gone?

She turned when she heard Haley come back outside. Haley's gaze went to the sun, which was sinking quickly behind the trees, then she handed over the drink to her.

"Thanks."

Haley said nothing as she continued to stare to the west.

"Is this a Sunday ritual? The sunset?"

"Yes. 'Seek the sound that never ceases. Seek the sun that never sets.'" Haley turned to her. "Rumi. My favorite quote of his."

She nodded. "A sound that continues. A sun that's always shining. Everything stays the same. Nothing changes."

Haley let out a deep breath. "But things do change, don't they? The sun always sets."

Carter followed her gaze, the sun now gone from view. "Why were you crying earlier?"

Haley didn't look at her. She kept her gaze to the west, the sky turning a gentle orange color. She took a sip of her wine before answering.

"Is saying I was feeling lonely too simple?" Haley turned to look at her. "Everything feels all messed up. Two murders? Of tourists, no less. The very thing that keeps this town alive.

And Mike? I'm worried about him." She looked back at the darkening sky. "But mostly I was feeling...alone. Lonely."

"Yes."

Haley gave her a sad smile. "You too, huh?"

"For a bunch of different reasons. I feel lonely for a home, but it's not something I ever had. My apartment was just the place I stayed. It wasn't a home." She took a sip of her drink. "And I feel lonely for companionship, which is strange. I never had that either. Everything was the job. Always. Partners came and went. Friendships started, then fizzled out, but there was always the job. It never failed me." She sighed. "Until it did."

Haley leaned forward, her elbows resting on her thighs, the wineglass held in both hands. "Are you happy, Carter?"

She hesitated only a beat before answering. "No. Are you?"

Haley smiled, then gave a quick laugh. "God, we're a pair, aren't we?"

"Tomorrow's my birthday."

"Yes. Should we celebrate? That has to be better than how I normally spend that day."

She arched an eyebrow. "Celebrate? That'll certainly be different for me."

Haley leaned back again, then slowly turned her head to look at her. She could see the misting of tears in Haley's eyes.

"I'm so lonely, Carter."

She held her gaze. "Do you want me to stay with you tonight?"

Haley wiped a tear away. "Stay?"

"Yes, stay. Sleep with you. Hold you."

As the shadows crept over them and the air chilled, she could see the indecision in Haley's eyes, could see that she was warring with herself. She supposed that's why the words Haley said next surprised her.

"Would you make love to me? Can you make me feel something, Carter?"

Now the indecision was hers. Would she be a fill-in for Gail? Would Haley be angry with her tomorrow? Would she think that Carter had taken advantage of her? *Was* she taking advantage of her? Or would Haley feel weak and cheated and be angry with herself? Those questions drifted away because the terribly haunted, lonely look in Haley's eyes made the decision for her.

"Yes."

CHAPTER TWENTY-EIGHT

By the time they left the deck and made their way through the dark house to her bedroom, Haley nearly changed her mind a half a dozen times. But she didn't. She was tired of crying, tired of being lonely. Tired of being *alone*. But was she using Carter? Was that fair?

It wasn't until they were actually *in* her bedroom that apprehension turned to fear. Gail was the only person she'd ever been intimate with. Eight years ago, at that. Carter seemed to sense her hesitation.

"If it's not what you want, just say so. I'll still stay the night. I'll still hold you."

"Why, Carter?" It was too dark in the room to see her eyes, but she thought she saw Carter smile.

"Because you need someone—me. It doesn't have to be about sex, Haley."

Haley nodded. "Okay. Then yes. Maybe I'd like you to just stay. To just hold me."

"I can do that."

She was surprised to feel a soft hand touch her cheek. She closed her eyes.

"I'm tired. It'll be good to sleep." Carter let her hand fall away. "It'll be good to be with someone."

Haley nodded, realizing that Carter wanted—needed—this too. This closeness with another person. Not necessarily sex, no. Just a presence. Just arms holding, hands touching. She finally moved then, going to the bed. She didn't need a light. She knew her way. She pulled the covers back and stripped off her clothes. She heard Carter doing the same.

She crawled under the covers, waiting. Carter went around to the opposite side. She felt the bed shift as Carter lay down beside her. Their hands touched first. Fingers brushing, then clasping. She relaxed and closed her eyes. She wasn't alone.

For the first time in eight years, she wasn't alone.

CHAPTER TWENTY-NINE

Carter was deliciously tangled with a warm body when her phone jarred her awake. It was Jason's ringtone. and she blindly reached out from under the covers to find her phone.

"It's the middle of the night, Jason," she mumbled.

"Oh, sorry, Agent Carter. I forgot about the time difference. But yes, it's early here too. Six."

"That means it's four here." She finally opened her eyes when she felt Haley shift beside her. "You got something?"

"I think I do. I emailed you a file. Found something in one of Goodson's old cases."

"Let me guess. You hacked their system?"

"Of course not. We work with them enough that I have clearance. Anyway, read the file. Call me if you want to discuss it. But I'm confident this is the guy you're looking for."

"Guy?" She leaned up on an elbow. "We're looking for a woman."

"No. I don't think so."

Much like Murdock, the call ended without any further remarks. She dropped the phone beside her on the bed, then rolled to her side, snaking her arm across Haley's waist as she rested her head against her shoulder.

"Who was that?" Haley asked quietly.

"Jason. He said he found something. One of Mike's old cases from LA."

"So you have to go?"

Carter closed her eyes. "No. Another hour or so."

She felt Haley take her hand and pull her arm more firmly around her. She smiled against her skin but said nothing. The hour passed quickly, though. This time it was Haley's phone that woke them—an alarm. She heard Haley groan as she silenced it.

"Time for work."

She could see the lightening sky through the blinds though the darkness was still thick inside. Was it five thirty? Earlier? She rolled to her back and stretched her legs out. She'd slept like a rock.

"Come to the saloon for breakfast later?"

"I guess it depends on what Jason sent me."

Haley sat up. "You're not going to leave town, are you?"

She smiled at the tiny bit of panic she heard in Haley's voice. "Don't think so." She sat up too and rubbed her face. "I slept great. You?"

"Surprisingly so. Thank you, Carter. It was nice not to wake up alone."

"My pleasure."

"And happy birthday."

She laughed quietly. "Oh, yeah. I'm another year older today, aren't I?" Her smile disappeared then. "Are you okay?" she asked gently. She heard Haley take in a deep breath before answering, although she couldn't quite make out her features in the shadows.

"This is always the loneliest day of my life. I think about her all the time, but this is the day I let her absence affect me the most, I guess. Then tomorrow I start all over on getting through another year."

"You don't have to be alone, Haley. There's no need to punish yourself because she died."

"Is that what I'm doing?"

"Isn't it?"

"Who am I going to let in, Carter? You? Should I let you in? I almost did last night, didn't I?"

"Yes. Almost."

"Yes. What if I had? Then what? When you leave, you think I'll be all better then?"

"You were twenty-six when she died. You're thirty-three. Haven't you given her enough years?"

Haley got out of bed quickly, unmindful of her nakedness. "Jesus, your bedside manner sucks, Carter."

The slamming of a door—the bathroom, she supposed—was fierce enough to rattle the window. With a sigh, she got out of bed too. *Yeah, your bedside manner does suck.* Haley was obviously angry or hurt...or both. She had no clue how to fix it. She wasn't going to apologize, though. If Haley wanted to waste her life, that was her business, but she had no intention of pretending it was perfectly normal to do so.

She got dressed, then pocketed her phone. She paused at the bathroom door before leaving. The shower was running so she simply turned and left the bedroom, closing the door behind her. She went out the front door, pausing to look around a bit. The sky was a light blue, but the sun was still hidden behind the mountains. She took a deep breath, savoring the freshness of the air before walking down Haley's driveway and onto the little trail that would take her back to Mike's place.

When she went inside, the smell of coffee greeted her. Mike was sitting at the table, drumming his fingers on its surface, apparently waiting for her.

"Well, look at you," he drawled with a grin. "Get lucky last night?"

"Hardly. I was companionship, nothing more." She went to the coffee, pouring herself a cup. "Today's the anniversary of Gail's death. It's a rough day for Haley."

"Really? I don't guess she's ever told me when she died. Good you were there then."

Carter nodded. "I suppose. Got a call though. Got some news."

"Oh, yeah? From the lab?"

"No. Jason." She set her coffee cup down on the table. "Let me get my laptop. We can look at it together. He found something in an old case of yours."

"I can't imagine what. I don't remember there being any overly dramatic cases."

Carter shrugged. "We'll see."

She brought her laptop back from the spare bedroom and set it up on the table. Mike scooted his chair around to her side and they sat together, shoulders brushing, as she pulled up her email. There were two from Jason, one from earlier that morning—with an attachment—and another one only a half hour ago. She opened the earlier one first.

"Edward Dickenson," Mike murmured. "Doesn't ring a bell."

She opened the file, and they both scanned it silently. Edward Dickenson, age twenty-four at the time, was originally arrested for the murder of his son, six-year-old Dillon Dickenson. The boy was found in his home, beaten, bloody and bruised. Arresting officer was Mike Goodson. The kid had a broken neck. Mother was hysterical and so on. She felt Mike stiffen beside her.

"Ring a bell now?"

"Yeah. But if I remember, it was a he-said, she-said type of thing and the prosecutor didn't have enough to charge either of them."

"You arrested the father, not the mother. Sheila Dickenson."

"Right. The mother was screaming and crying and was deathly afraid of the guy. He was just standing there staring at the kid, I remember." Mike shook his head. "That was a couple of years before I left. Hell, more than twelve now, I guess. I don't remember everything, but I arrested him on the spot, yeah. He had blood on his hands."

She nodded, reading more of the file out loud. "Mother gave a play-by-play of what happened, indicting the father. After further questioning, the father gave a different account. Bruising around the boy's neck seemed to match the mother's hands but was inconclusive. Ultimately they couldn't prove either of them killed him, so both were eventually convicted of a lesser charge—child endangerment—and sentenced to eight years." She glanced at him. "This was after you'd already quit the force."

Mike leaned back in his chair. "Okay, so what makes your guy Jason think this case is related?"

"Let's read his notes." She pointed to the screen. "Here. Look here. The book."

Mike leaned up again. "*Alone With the Bears*. Book was found clutched in the boy's hand. Could be coincidence."

"Highly doubtful."

"So then what the hell does this mean? The mother is now taking out her revenge on me. Hell, I thought the father did it. I arrested *him*, not her."

"Get this. They both got released last year. Mother went to live with her sister in LA. Father moved to Vegas. According to Jason, the mother went missing two months ago. No sign of her since. Father was still in Vegas up until one month ago. Twenty-six days to be exact. Quit his job—he worked at a hotel doing maintenance—and left town. Hasn't resurfaced."

"I don't get it. Why is he so sure this is linked? I mean, I get the book thing, sure, but why would that mother be up here after me? Like I said, I didn't arrest her. I was already gone when their trial came up."

"Not her. Him."

Mike frowned. "What?"

"Him. Jason thinks the father—Edward Dickenson—has the beef with you. Look here, it's his work ID. Long hair, pulled back in a ponytail. Brunette," she said pointedly.

"But…" His brows drew together tightly. "*What*? He thinks the brunette…no way."

Carter smiled at him. "Yeah. He thinks the brunette was a dude."

Mike nearly knocked his chair over as he stood. "No fucking way! She...she was a *she*. She flirted with me. Hell, she kissed me!" He ran a hand through his hair. "Granted, her voice was a little husky. She didn't have long nails or anything, and they were painted an odd color. Not black but like dark blue or something." Mike met her gaze. "Oh Christ. You think she was a he?"

"From what I saw, she had a whole lot of makeup on, like maybe trying to hide a beard. Stubble, you know."

"Oh, Christ."

"I think it makes sense. Look," she pointed to the screen. "He maintained his innocence throughout. Said the mother did it. Said she always beat the kid." She leaned back in the chair. "So say he is innocent. He just spent eight years in prison for something he didn't do. He's pissed. You're the one who arrested him."

"Hell, but I didn't prosecute him. Why is he coming after me?"

"He left the knife and the body in your Jeep. He's trying to frame you. Payback."

"And the mother? Where does she fit in?"

Carter opened the second email from Jason, reading it quickly. "Not only the mother who is missing. Eric Crumpton, assistant district attorney." She glanced at him. "He was the prosecutor. Last seen leaving his office on May fourth. Never made it home. His vehicle was found abandoned on the side of the highway."

"Shit. Dickenson's wife is not missing—"

"He killed her," they said in unison.

"And most likely Eric Crumpton too," Carter added.

Mike sat down heavily in his chair. "I was drugged. He had the knife. Why not off me too?"

"He wanted to frame you. Make you spend time for something you didn't do."

"I can't believe this is happening to me." He stood up again. "Why is he leaving the book? Does he think it won't lead back to him?"

"Maybe he doesn't care."

"If he's trying to frame me, why leave anything that might lead back to him?"

"Maybe he doesn't know the book was logged in as evidence. Maybe because it's been over ten years, he doesn't think it'll trace back to him."

"If a prosecutor goes missing, that's the first thing they do. Go back to old cases."

Carter nodded. "Right. But how long would it take to weed through them all? And is there anything about this case that stands out more than others?"

"If he hadn't left the book, Jason wouldn't have linked it either. Right?"

"Hard to say," she said with a shrug. "He puts all this stuff into one of his algorithms. Who knows what he's looking for? Or what he'll find."

Mike nodded. "Okay. Now what?"

"Now we—" Her phone interrupted, and she pulled it out of her pocket. "It's the lab. Yeah, Carter here."

"Agent Carter, it's me. Zach. Got some things I thought you might be interested in."

"Great. Give it to me."

"Let's start with the easy stuff first. Prints on the book come back to Mike Goodson, your police chief there. The prints were clean. No blood, no smears. Perfect, in fact."

"Staged."

"Yes, like the prints on the knife. Too perfect. Oh, and the blood on the knife—it matches Trevor Greene, our victim. Perfect frame job." He paused. "That is what you're thinking, right? Chief Goodson is not a suspect, is he?"

She glanced at Mike. "He's not a suspect. What else you got?"

"Blood under our victim's nails is not a match to him. It's male, however. We're running it, hoping to get a hit. I did run it against Mike Goodson's DNA, to be sure. Not a match to him either. Also, the hair samples came back male, not female. It matched the blood under the vic's nails. So if we get a hit in the system—"

"You will. Edward Dickenson. Thanks, Zach. And what about the Jeep?"

"Yes, it's here. That's next on my list."

"Great. And what about tox?"

"Not yet."

"Okay. Let me know when you get DNA confirmation, please."

"Will do, Agent Carter."

She put her phone down beside her laptop. "Your prints were on the book. Blood on the knife belonged to the victim, Trevor Greene. But blood under his nails didn't belong to him. Unknown male." She smiled. "The brunette hair samples—male."

Mike shook his head. "I don't get it. Why pretend to be a woman?"

"All three victims were young. Trevor Greene being only nineteen. So you pretend to be a woman and offer them sex. Who's going to turn it down?" She laughed. "Hell, you were no better. You were gonna sleep with her. *Him*," she corrected.

Mike's face remained serious. "Let's don't tell anyone this, okay? Not even Haley."

"She's probably not speaking to me anyway. I kinda pissed her off."

"How so? I thought you stayed with her for companionship or whatever the hell excuse you made."

She nodded. "Yeah. I was going to sleep with her." She grinned. "Like…you know."

"Have sex? With Haley?"

"Yeah. But she changed her mind, so I just stayed the night. She didn't want to be alone."

"How'd you piss her off then?"

"Told her she'd wasted enough years on this woman. Something like that."

"Oh, Carter. Probably not your best move."

"Yeah, well the truth hurts." She picked up her phone. "Let me call Jason."

CHAPTER THIRTY

Haley looked up as Mike came in, then automatically glanced behind him. There was no Carter. Just as well, she supposed. She wasn't in the mood to talk to her anyway. She plastered a smile on her face when Mike sat down.

"Good morning," she said with forced cheerfulness. "You're too late for the good coffee."

Mike arched an eyebrow. "Why are you pissed at Carter?"

The forced smile disappeared. "And good morning to you too."

"She told me why you were pissed, but what's the real reason?"

"The real reason?" She slid a cup in front of him and filled it with coffee. "You don't think that's reason enough?"

He arched an eyebrow at her. "Is it?" Then he held a hand up. "None of my business, I guess."

"Where is she? Is she scared to come around now?"

"She dropped me off. She went on to the station. She needed

to call Zach about something." He took a sip of the coffee. "My prints were on the damn book."

"The book?"

"Yeah, they found another book in my Jeep, same as the others. So my prints are on the murder weapon and now on the book that was left with the body. Oh, and the blood on the knife—Trevor Greene's."

"Oh, Mike, no. Surely Carter doesn't think you did anything, right?"

"No. But it's freaking me out all the same. I mean, this guy drugged me. He had the knife. He could have killed me like that," he said, snapping his fingers together. "Yet let's frame Mike Goodson instead. That'll be fun."

Haley frowned. "He? I thought you were looking for that woman. The brunette you were with."

"Oh, shit," he murmured. He rubbed his forehead, then looked around. They were alone at the bar and only three tables were occupied. "Look, it appears that she…well, that she was a he. A dude."

"*What?*"

"Yeah. A guy. And please don't tell anybody. I mean, she kissed me," he nearly hissed, pointing to the table where they'd been sitting. "Right there!"

Haley couldn't help the laughter that popped up. "You mean, *he* kissed you?"

Mike groaned. "Can you believe it? Me? Getting duped like that? Christ!"

She leaned her elbows on the bar. "So this guy pretended to be a woman. For what purpose?"

"Carter thinks to get close to those guys, offer them sex. Then she—*he*—drugs them. Then kills them. Same with me. Some dude wasn't going to get close enough to spike my drink. But a woman did."

"Then why did he kill those guys and not you? I mean, that's good for you and all, but—"

"He's trying to frame me. Long story. It's some guy from my past, in LA. An old case. Or at least that's the way it's looking."

"So he's not trying to kill you? That's comforting, at least."

"Carter says he will try to kill me when he realizes that I'm not being arrested. I think she plans on being my bodyguard or something. Hell, like I need a goddamn babysitter."

She laughed. "You got picked up at a bar by a guy pretending to be a woman. Yeah, you probably need a babysitter." She touched his hand. "But really, she thinks this guy is still hanging around Timber Falls?"

"Maybe he's camping somewhere back in the woods."

"How is she going to find him? She's working by herself."

"I don't even pretend to know anything about what she does. This guy Jason takes all of this information and 'runs it' or something. But, yeah, she's alone. Well, there's me, you know. And she said something about Murdock—he's her boss—sending in another team to help her. She didn't seem happy about that."

"Is she like, *real* FBI, Mike?"

"Not like any FBI I've worked with before, but yes, she's real." He motioned to the kitchen. "Better get a couple of tacos. I'll take her breakfast. She probably didn't have dinner last night." Then he arched an eyebrow. "Or did she?"

"Not with me, no."

He held her gaze. "It sucks being alone all the time, Haley. We both know that. Might do you good to let Carter into your life."

"Let her into my life? I think I already have. She slept in my bed last night."

"You know what I mean, Haley."

She sighed. "For what reason, Mike? I let her in. Then what? She'll be leaving. Sooner rather than later, I imagine. What purpose would it serve to get involved with her?"

"Maybe just to let you know that you're the one still alive, Haley."

"I know I'm still alive. Every day, I know that I'm still here and she's not."

She hurried into the kitchen, glancing only briefly at CeCe. "Four tacos. Chorizo, with cheese. For Mike." Then she went out the back door, letting it slam shut behind her.

Yes, she was alive. Of course she knew that. What scared her though was that she couldn't see Gail's face clearly anymore. Her expressions. The brightness of her eyes. Her smile. They weren't as fresh, as vibrant. She stared up into the blue sky, trying to find Gail's face. What came was a still shot, one of the pictures she kept out in her bedroom—a picture of the two of them at a friend's birthday party. It was one of the few pictures she had. Oh, there were others, most of Gail on her hiking trips. Haley could always tell the difference in her eyes in those pictures. Gail was *in love* with her sport. She could see that in her eyes. Maybe that's why she'd never printed out any of those pictures. She didn't *want* to see that in Gail's eyes. No. What she saw instead was them at a birthday party, smiling. Yes, they were smiling. She remembered the party, though. It had been on a Saturday, and she had forced Gail to go, forced Gail to miss a hike. And while Gail pretended to have a good time, Haley could see the difference in her eyes.

Now when she thought of Gail, that's what she saw. Them in that picture. Gail smiling at the camera. Gail wishing she was out on a mountain peak instead of there at a party with their friends. And her.

"Oh, Christ." She balled her hands into fists. They were *happy*. Weren't they? Yes, of course. They had a good relationship. They always had. Yet wasn't there constantly a longing in Gail's eyes? Like she was still searching for something. Had she ever found it? Had she found it on top of a fourteen-thousand-foot mountain? Did that longing disappear when she was up there?

Gail wasn't around to ask, no. But did she need to ask? All she had to do was to look at one of those photos her climbing partner had sent her. She knew the answer. It stared her right in the face when she looked into Gail's eyes.

CHAPTER THIRTY-ONE

"What I don't get," Carter said as she paced slowly in Mike's office, "is why kill those three guys?" She shifted her cell to her other ear. "Especially the one in Albuquerque."

"You can't try to reason out the thinking of a serial killer," Murdock said.

"Is he a serial killer? I mean, technically, yeah, he is. But if Jason is right, this is about revenge. He kills his wife, he kills the prosecutor. Why not just kill the cop who arrested you too?" She nodded to herself. "But okay, I get that. What better revenge than to make that same cop spend time in prison for a crime he didn't do?"

"Keep in mind that it's only an assumption that he killed the wife and prosecutor."

"Right. But still, is he trying to tie all three of these recent killings to Mike? Is that the purpose of the books?"

"What are you thinking?"

"I don't know. He spent eight years locked up. You're angry, thinking you're innocent. You want revenge, sure. But then you kill. You kill your wife first. And maybe it dimmed your anger some. Then you kill the prosecutor. You still have this anger. Maybe killing him helps assuage it, but maybe not. So then he devises a plan for Mike. Frame him for one killing? Hell, let's frame him for three."

"Because he now likes killing?"

"The killings have been violent, angry. Yeah, I think he likes them, but maybe it's something else too. The first two, especially, were mutilated. It was more than just a killing. It was rage." She paused, frowning. "I think we need to look at his prison records. Was he raped? Maybe repeatedly? That could explain the violence."

"Okay, I'll check into it. Now where is he? Did he kill and then disappear, hoping Mike Goodson will take the fall?"

"No. I think he sticks around. I think—if Mike is still walking around a free man—he tries to kill him."

"Is there a BOLO out on his car? What about his phone?"

"The last hit on his phone was a cell tower in Vegas over a month ago. Nothing since. And yes, there's a BOLO. But I'm guessing he ditched his car. You don't go on a murder spree using your own vehicle."

"Does Jason concur?"

Carter only barely resisted rolling her eyes. "He hasn't gotten back with me. But my gut says—"

"Let's wait for Jason. In the meantime, since Reynolds was already in Vegas, I've got his team looking into Edward Dickenson and trying to trace his steps going back to when his wife went missing. There's got to be a gap there if he went to LA to kill her. I've also got his guy Rowan looking into the wife's disappearance. That was a case that went nowhere. Maybe Rowan can dig up something. I'll have him check into his prison records too. We'll talk soon."

She stared at her phone as the screen went black. "Sure. We'll talk," she murmured. "In the meantime...what?" With a sigh, she tossed her phone onto Mike's desk. Well, in the meantime, she supposed she'd be Mike's shadow.

She sat down at his desk and pulled up the file Jason had sent her, wanting to read through it again. It made perfect sense. It had to be this guy. But where the hell was he?

CHAPTER THIRTY-TWO

It wasn't until the lunch crowd had come and gone that Haley realized how sparse it had been. In fact, they'd had empty tables even out on the patio. And to say that the patrons had been subdued was an understatement. Very little jubilant laughter was heard, and conversations had been quiet and passive.

She moved down the bar to where Bill was still sitting, drinking the last of his mug of beer. His plate was empty, not even a smear remaining of the ketchup that he'd doused his steak fries with. She leaned on the bar close to him.

"Kinda quiet in town today, huh?"

He nodded quickly. "I'll say."

She leaned closer. "What have you heard?"

"Heard they're shutting the campgrounds down. People have to be out by dark."

"So they're really doing it? I bet Sam is throwing a fit over that."

"Oh, you know he is. Heard practically everyone booked to run the river today canceled."

She looked through the window to the river. "I guess I hadn't noticed the lack of rafts coming by."

"The RV park is not closing, though," he continued. "Of course, not many of them run the river each day like those kids do." He tapped his finger on the bar. "Haven't seen those deputies out and about. Shouldn't they be up here looking for a killer?"

"From what I understand, the FBI is on the case, not the sheriff's department."

"FBI? What? That one gal?"

Haley shrugged. "Don't know about that. Mike said something about a team joining her."

He looked around as if making sure they were alone. "Heard something else."

"Oh, yeah?"

"Heard that FBI woman has been staying over at Mike's place. Him there too with her." He leaned closer. "Speculation going around is that they're having an affair."

Haley couldn't hide her smile. "An affair? With Carter?" She shook her head. "No. There's no affair. Trust me."

Bill shoved his empty mug toward her, indicating he'd like a refill. She dutifully took it over to the tap.

"Scott didn't think there was an affair either. He said Mike wasn't her type, if you know what I mean," Bill said.

Haley put his spent mug in the basin and got a frosty one from the freezer.

"Said maybe *you* were her type."

Haley stared at him. What was going on? First Sylvia, now Butter Bill was making innuendos about her personal life.

She placed a fresh mug in front of him. "Is that what he said?"

Bill nodded as he took a big swallow of his beer. "She's kinda cute, I guess. You could do worse."

"Well, thank you, Bill. I'll keep that in mind."

She turned and grabbed the pitcher of tea, taking it over to one of the tables and mindlessly refilling their glasses. Why were they pushing Carter on her? After all these years, why now did they think they needed to be involved in her personal life?

Well, maybe because there hadn't been an opportunity before. That wasn't really true, though. The third summer, one of the college students she'd hired had made it no secret that she was interested in her. She smiled at the memory. Marlin. Her name had been Marlin. She flirted incessantly with her. And sure, she was cute, but Haley hadn't been tempted in the least. She'd still been too raw over Gail's death to even begin to contemplate it.

And yes, she'd been flirted with by tourists from time to time. Again, she laughed it off, never giving it a consideration at all. None of the locals ever made mention of it either.

Now Carter. Did Carter flirt with her? A little, yes. Coming by to help her cook. Teasing with her. Talking with her. She'd shared some things with Carter that she'd not mentioned to anyone else, not even her mother. She enjoyed Carter's company and certainly liked talking to her.

But was she attracted to her? She must be—at least a little—since she'd asked her to sleep with her. Not sleep, no. That hadn't been her intention.

"Would you make love to me? Can you make me feel something, Carter?"

Carter had been so sweet, hadn't she? Sweet and understanding. They'd shared a bed and Carter had held her, making her feel safe. Making her feel a part of something—someone. Helping to ease her loneliness, if only for a night.

More than a night. Here it was, the anniversary of Gail's death and she wasn't eaten up with loneliness, eaten up with what-ifs. She wasn't dwelling on her past like she normally did on this date. She wasn't dreading the future and the emptiness it held.

No, she was trying to decide if she was pissed at Carter or attracted to her. And she couldn't decide if that made her feel happy...or sad.

CHAPTER THIRTY-THREE

"You think this guy knows where I live?"

"I'm sure he does." Carter stopped in front of Mike's desk and pointed at the still-stripped bed. "He certainly knew you slept here at the station."

"So he's been in town watching me? That would be easy enough to get lost in the crowd. And it's not like we've got any surveillance cameras around. Bobby's got one over at the gas station. They've got one inside the post office. That's about all I can think of."

"The photo Jason sent was his work ID. That was the most recent photo he could find. But he's midthirties. Not old, certainly, but not blending in as easily as the college students do." She sat down in a chair. "You know what I think?"

He raised his eyebrows.

"Remember that first day when you were showing me around. You said that some guy reported the killing—well, reported the bloody tent."

Mike leaned forward. "Yeah. The older guy who probably wasn't camping there. You think it was him?"

"Maybe. He kills Hayden Anderson in the early morning hours. Goes and washes up. Comes back around at daybreak."

Mike nodded. "Anderson goes into the tent sometime after midnight. That's when his friends said the party broke up. So our guy—pretending to be a woman—waits until everything quiets down, then goes into the tent."

Carter nodded. "Anderson has been drinking. He may already be asleep. Our guy wakes him up, flirts with him, offers sex."

"But hey, let's have a drink first."

"Exactly. Spikes the drink. If he'd been drinking for hours, it probably didn't take long for him to pass out."

Mike rubbed the stubble on his chin. "I'll buy it. Does it help?"

"Not really, no."

"So is there a plan? Are we going to go out and scour the woods, looking for his camp?"

"I think we should. He must have a vehicle. Are there places to camp that are off the beaten path yet still accessible by car?"

"Not car, but an SUV or truck, sure. In the Timber Falls area, we have three forest service roads that go into the backcountry. You can camp anywhere off any of them. Got a few crude roads too, from long ago logging."

"Permits needed to camp?"

"No. They allow fourteen-day camping, then you're supposed to move on. The forest service is pretty good about moving them along."

"Do a lot of people do that?"

"Boondock?" Mike grinned. "That's what it's called when you camp away from a managed campground. Anyway, yeah, there's a few. It's free camping and you don't have all the rules of a campground. You also don't have water or bathrooms and such. But these college kids, they don't care so much. They'll pitch a tent anywhere and sleep for free. They just piss in the woods."

"Okay, so yeah, then let's take a look around tomorrow. Might get lucky."

"That SUV of yours is four-wheel drive?"

"It is."

"Good. Then we can go pretty much everywhere. Hell, Carter, I'll show you around the area. You might fall in love with it."

"Speaking of falling in love, I'm thinking one of those chicken-fried steaks over at the saloon sound good. Early dinner?"

He laughed. "An excuse to go see Haley?"

She smiled at him. "I like her. And speaking of that, maybe we should sleep at her place tonight."

"Whatever for?"

"Because like you said, he knows where you live."

"We're cops, Carter. You don't think we can handle him if he tries to come after me?"

"Why take that chance?"

"Maybe he doesn't come after me. He wants to frame me, remember?"

"I think if he knows you've not been arrested, then at some point, he has to consider that we know who he is. He wants revenge. He'll try to kill you. I don't think he cares about being caught. He's only after revenge. If he has to go back to prison, he probably doesn't care. In his eyes, his life is over with anyway. He probably felt that way the day you arrested him."

"Let me guess…you were a psychology major, and you wanted to be a police profiler."

She laughed. "Good guess. Both are true. I also have spent a lot of time on a shrink's couch."

"Oh yeah? Willingly or department mandated?"

"The latter."

He met her gaze. "You kill someone?"

She swallowed. "Three." Then she held her hand up. "Don't want to talk about it, though. So? Sleep at Haley's?"

"Do we really want to get her involved?"

"If we tell her that we think our killer is hiding somewhere out here in these woods, she'd probably welcome the company."

"I don't know. I thought she was mad at you."

"Surely she's over that by now. Come on, let's go get a beer. You can listen to everyone bitch about the tourists leaving town."

"Oh, man, you should have heard Sam. It was like he was blaming me for the campgrounds closing."

"We don't know what this guy's motives are anymore. Is he just after you or will he kill again? Better to be safe and get those campers out of here."

"This town's living is made during the summer months. Even if this wraps up early, who's to say they come back? These are young kids, still under their parents' thumb. Hell, if I had a kid, I wouldn't want them near Timber Falls."

"It'll pass, Mike. People will forget about the killings. It'll be a footnote." She motioned to the door. "Come on."

Jewell was wrapping up for the day too. She nodded at them as she slung her purse over her shoulder. "Kinda quiet in town today."

"Yeah, it was," Mike said. "Probably going to get quieter too. Those campgrounds hold hundreds of people each."

"Not only that," Jewell said. "Sherry came over to visit. Sherry owns the shop next door," she explained to her. "She heard that people left the lodge in droves too."

"Damn. You'd think they'd feel safe there," Mike said. "Can't say I blame them, though."

"The fewer people around, the easier it'll be to find him," Carter said.

"Don't reckon we'll ever see a June day as quiet as tomorrow will be," Jewell said with a nod at both of them. "See you in the morning."

They followed her out, then Mike paused to lock the door. No cars traveled the normally busy street and only a handful of people were on the sidewalk, looking into shop windows. Yes, Timber Falls was quiet indeed.

"Carter, what if we don't find him? What if he packed up and left town? Then what?"

"He'll have to resurface somewhere. Jason will have programs running, looking for hits on his name, SSN, credit cards, things like that. If he left town, he'll pop up somewhere."

"Well, I for one hope he didn't leave town. I want to catch this bastard. I don't want to have to be looking over my shoulder for the next year, wondering when he's going to try to kill me."

"For what it's worth, I think he's still around. Unfinished business."

"Yeah, he's probably kicking himself that he didn't kill me when he had the chance." Mike shook his head. "That poor kid. I can't help but feel responsible. Hell, three of them. Innocent kids up here for a good time. Then—"

"Mike, you've been a cop for a long time. The blame lies with the killer. The circumstances that set it in motion are just that, a string of events that no one could control. It's not your fault."

CHAPTER THIRTY-FOUR

Haley tried to temper the smile on her face when Mike and Carter came through the door. Temper it because she wasn't sure if she should still be mad at Carter or not. Of course, if she had to question it, she knew she probably wasn't. Slightly annoyed, maybe. No, not really even that. She took two mugs from the freezer and began drawing beer before either of them had sat down.

The only people at the bar were Scott, Bill, and Charlie. The normal boisterous crowd was missing. There were no stories being told of how they'd managed Dead Man Falls or how they'd taken a spill. No one fighting for a spot on the outdoor patio. It was quite subdued in fact. Only two tables were occupied and even then, the guests looked nervous. Butter Bill's ominous prediction that the town would be deserted by tomorrow seemed to be coming true.

She brought the mugs over, casually meeting Carter's gaze before turning to Mike. "How are you holding up? Heard Sam gave you an earful today."

"Yeah, he did. His bitching to the forest service was ignored so he thought he'd try me." He took a swallow of his beer. "I guess rightfully so."

Carter nudged him. "The three of us are the only ones who know your connection to this guy. Let's keep it that way."

"I agree," she said, keeping her voice as quiet as Carter's. "You're certainly not to blame for what's going on, Mike."

"I appreciate that, but let's be real. The only reason he's in Timber Falls is because of me." He glanced behind him. "Look around. It'll be like a ghost town tomorrow."

"And if there are no more murders, the tourists will come back." Carter met her gaze. "Can we talk somewhere? Private."

Haley was surprised at the seriousness of her tone, her expression. "Okay. I have a small office."

She walked around the bar, heading to the little room that served as her office. It had once been a closet, but Eddie had told her he'd knocked out the side wall of the spandrel under the stairs to enlarge it. Even so, it was barely large enough for a desk and the small table that held her printer. There was one visitor's chair in the corner, and she went to it, picking up the stack of inventory papers that had been collecting there.

"Are you still mad at me?"

She turned, still holding the papers in her hands. "Was I mad?"

"You slammed that door awfully hard."

"So I did," she agreed. "I guess I was mad at the time." She went around her desk, placing the stack of papers on top of the printer. "I'm over it. Besides, I should thank you."

Carter stood in front her desk. "Thank me for what?"

"For taking my mind off the significance of this day. To be honest, I've thought more about you today than Gail." The truth of that shocked her, to be sure. "And yes, I was upset with you."

"But now you're not?"

"No." She looked away, then back. "What you said was the truth. That didn't make it sting any less. Today, of all days, is when I allow some self-pity—usually a lot." She waved a hand. "Wallow in my misery and all that. Instead, I was thinking of you and how sweet you were last night, and instead of thanking you properly, I slammed a door in your face."

A smile played on Carter's lips. "A proper thank-you would have been what? A kiss? You can thank me now if you like."

Haley's gaze lowered to Carter's mouth. She'd kissed two women in her life—Kelly and Gail. Kelly was but a distant memory but what surprised her was that she could no longer remember Gail's kiss either. Her earlier fears came back to her—she couldn't *see* Gail anymore. What if she gave in to her loneliness? What if she let Carter in? Would Gail disappear completely? Would a couple of old photos be all she had?

Would that be so bad? What had Carter said to her that morning? Hadn't she given Gail enough years? Had she?

"I didn't really come in here to talk about kissing, though."

Haley blinked several times, pulling her eyes from Carter's mouth. She smiled a bit apologetically, then sat down. "No, I don't guess you did."

Carter sat down too, but she leaned forward, her elbows resting on her thighs. "Need a favor. For me and Mike."

"Of course. Anything."

Carter nodded. "I'd like for us to stay at your house tonight. I don't know that our guy would be so bold as to break into Mike's house, but I thought it would be better not to give him that opportunity. Our thinking is that he's camping somewhere up here, hiding." She leaned back against the chair. "Jason is running some stuff for me. He downloaded topo maps of the area. Mike and I are going out in the morning. With so many campers leaving the area, we're hoping we might get lucky and run into this guy."

"Okay, sure. Of course you can stay. That's no problem."

"Mike says you've hiked all over up here. Says you know the trails."

She nodded. "Yes. When the tourists leave in September until the snow hangs around, I'm out nearly every day. Why? How does that help you?"

"Do you know of any out of the way places that maybe the forest rangers wouldn't check on? Any hidden campsites?"

"There are a few places, yes. I'm assuming you mean where you could drive a vehicle to, right?"

"Yes."

"Okay, yeah, I can think of a few. I've got a trail map at the house. We can go over it tonight if you want. Or in the morning."

Carter smiled. "Great. I know Jason will give me some suggestions, but I thought it would be more accurate if it came from someone who has actually been there." She stood up. "What time can you leave tonight?"

"Seeing as how there's not much of a crowd, I can leave anytime."

"Great. Then we'll do an early dinner and get out of here."

CHAPTER THIRTY-FIVE

Mike laughed as she pulled a bottle of whiskey from a paper bag. "You brought us a present?"

"Swiped it from the bar," Haley said, placing the bottle on the kitchen counter. "Carter had a glass last night, so the bottle you left here is about empty."

"Carter had a glass, huh?" He glanced over his shoulder as if making sure they were still alone. "She grows on you, doesn't she?"

"Yes. I like her." She took two glasses down and a wineglass for herself. "Did you know today is her birthday?"

"Really? I thought today was…well, she said—"

"Yes. Gail died on this date. Kinda ironic, don't you think?"

"Maybe it's fate."

She laughed lightly. "Do you believe in fate?"

"Do you?"

"Are we talking in the context of Gail's accident? Or the killings or what?" She shoved the glasses toward him then took down the bottle of whiskey that had maybe enough for one drink in it. "Those young men were simply at the wrong place, wrong time. Yes, I guess that would be fate. But Gail? That was an accident. I don't think you can call an accident fate. If you did, then it was almost like it was preordained to happen." She shrugged. "I guess the same could be said for the killings."

He poured whiskey into two glasses. "So not fate then?"

"I don't know. I guess at this point, does it matter?" She went to the fridge and took out the bottle of chardonnay she'd opened last night. "Let's go with bad luck or bad timing." She nearly filled her glass with wine. "Both are out of our control, aren't they?"

"And what about you and Carter?"

She paused, considering the question. "What about us? Fate again? Or a chance meeting?"

"Well, I didn't mean anything quite that deep. Just maybe an opportunity for you…well, to get past everything."

"Get past Gail? Get past my past?"

He picked up his tumbler and took a sip. "Yeah. Something like that."

She smiled at him, grasping his hand. "Are you hoping I have sex?"

He grinned back at her. "It would be nice if one of us did. Christ, it's been a while."

Her smile faltered a little. "I'm scared, I think. I've only been with Gail. So…"

"Really?"

"Really."

"Yeah, well, I can't help you there, kiddo. But if it were me, I'd go for it."

She laughed lightly. "You think it'll change things?"

"I think it's been a lot of years. Carter told me what she said to you. I have to agree. You've had a lot of wasted years, Haley. You'll wake up one day and be downright old and wonder where the time went."

"Oh, Mike, I've thought of that. I really have. But what can Carter offer me? She'll be gone in a matter of days, probably."

"She can—"

His words were cut off as Carter came into the kitchen, her hair still obviously damp from her shower. She was wearing shorts, not jeans and Haley found herself staring. She looked up then, meeting Carter's gaze. Whereas she may have expected there to be some teasing or even a gloating look for having caught her staring, there was neither. Carter's gaze was warm and perhaps a bit shy.

"Here. Have a drink with us," Mike offered, sliding a glass along the counter toward her. "Might even have two."

"Thanks."

Instead of standing at the counter like they were, Carter sat down at the small table, scooting her chair far enough away to stretch her legs out. Haley again found her gaze drawn to them and she mentally rolled her eyes at herself. Yes, she did, but that didn't stop her from recalling sleeping with Carter last night. Those bare legs had been between her own as Carter held her while she slept.

"Heard anything from Jason?" Mike asked.

"A brief email saying he'd have something for me in the morning. If it's not first thing, though, I'd still like us to head out and do some preliminary searching, if nothing else."

"I'm good with that. Do you think we should request the sheriff's department to send some deputies up here? I know there's only three forest service roads, but that's still a lot of ground to cover."

"Tell me about the old logging roads. If they're crude like you said, they're probably not used very often."

"They haven't logged this area in thirty years or more. Those roads were never maintained. Need a four-wheel-drive for sure, but no, they're not used much. Most don't really go anywhere, though."

"I know of one that's used more often," Haley said. "The one that goes on the east side of Cinnamon Creek. They didn't replant that area and there's still a good view of Timber Falls from there. Timber Falls meaning the falls, not the town," she explained to Carter. "Nice opportunity for photos."

"Yeah, but that's one of the shorter roads. Steep until you get to the top. The only camping would be out there in the open," Mike said.

"I wouldn't think our guy would camp somewhere where he's boxed in," Carter said. "If these logging roads all dead-end, then I don't think they should be of concern."

"Probably right," Mike said.

Carter's phone rang and her expression changed as she looked at it. "Reynolds," she said before answering. "Carter here."

Haley looked at Mike, wondering who Reynolds was. Mike shrugged.

Carter got up, nodding. "Yeah, let me get my laptop."

When she walked out, Haley raised her eyebrows. "Who is Reynolds?"

"I think that's the team that Murdock wanted to send in. Carter said they were working on the wife's disappearance, I think." Mike poured a little more whiskey into his glass. "Maybe they found something."

"Do you think we're safe here tonight?"

"What do you mean?"

"What if this guy was watching you today? Followed you over here? Maybe he—"

"No, no. Carter thought of that too. Hell, before we came over she drove in circles around town. Went downriver a ways, then back up past Sam's place. Hardly any cars on the road as it was. None followed us, that's for sure."

Carter came back in then, but she didn't have her laptop and her phone was apparently pocketed.

"That was Reynolds. I trained with him for about a month. Anyway, his team is in Vegas. They're looking into Dickenson's last days there. He said Rowan—that's his version of Jason— found when Dickenson went to LA. He stopped for gas at one of the truck stops on the way and again on the way back."

"You think he'd be smarter than to use a credit card."

"He didn't. Paid cash. Rowan got into their surveillance and ran some face recognition program. Anyway, based on when he was there fueling up, Rowan was able to estimate when he left Vegas, how long he was in LA and when he headed back."

"And it coincides with when the wife went missing or the prosecutor?" Mike asked.

Carter smiled. "The wife. Exact match. He also found his car. He sold it. It's sitting on a used car lot in Vegas."

"Buy a new one?"

"Not there, no. Rowan's still looking. My guess is he stole one."

"That's taking a chance," he said.

"Not as much as using your own car," Carter said. "Too easy to trace nowadays."

"What about his phone?" she asked.

Carter shook her head. "It's dark. Hasn't been on since early May. Jason is running a script, though. If he turns his phone on at any point, it'll show up."

"So is this team going to join you up here?" Mike asked.

"Reynolds said he hasn't been told to relocate yet. I'd just as soon they not. Reynolds is a team leader. He has seniority."

"Meaning he'd call the shots?"

"Most likely. He's very rigid, very by the book. We didn't really get along all that well."

"Then I hope he stays away. You and I can handle this." Mike held his glass up to her. "Cheers."

Carter nodded and took her glass, motioning it in his direction. "Cheers."

Haley smiled at the affection between them as she picked up her wineglass too, joining them in a toast. "Cheers," she echoed.

CHAPTER THIRTY-SIX

"You going to get any sleep tonight?" Carter asked as Mike drew back his 9-mil, loading a round into the chamber.

"The house is locked up tight. If he comes inside there'll be breaking glass. I'm sure we'll hear that. And if he tries to come through this window," he said, motioning to the lone one in the spare bedroom, "I'll drop him where he stands."

"I don't think we'll have any visitors during the night. Hopefully we can get some rest. I imagine tomorrow will be a long day."

When she turned to go, Mike called her back.

"Carter, I need to thank you."

"For what?"

"Well, for not locking my ass up, for one thing. But for, well, for letting me be your sidekick. I'm guessing it's not exactly part of the FBI's normal procedure."

Carter smiled at him. "That seems to be the problem. I don't really feel like I'm FBI. I have credentials that say I am, though, but really, I don't think this job is for me." She took a deep breath, surprised by the words. "I'm not used to waiting around, waiting on some computer genius to tell me where to go, what to look for. Not used to having a commander who lives across the country and only communicates with me by phone."

"You thinking about quitting?"

She shrugged. "Too soon to know, I guess. He wants me working out of a motorhome."

Mike frowned. "A what?"

"Yeah, apparently they've got some custom-built motorhome that Jason is connected to. I'm supposed to learn how to run his programs."

"Seriously?"

"Yes. Who knows? I may like that better. At least I wouldn't have to wait around on him. I could run them myself. It's the living and traveling in the motorhome part that's not appealing. Mainly because I don't know anything about it."

"Takes a certain kind, I suppose. Me? I like to put down roots."

She nodded. She'd never given it much thought one way or the other. She'd had an apartment that she called home, but it wasn't anything special. She wasn't tied to her family. She was no longer tied to her job in LA. She didn't have roots anywhere, did she? Maybe she should reconsider the motorhome. Maybe it would be fun. She let a quiet sigh escape at the thought.

"Good night, Mike."

"Good night." Then he winked. "Don't you girls stay up all night now. Got a busy day tomorrow."

She smiled as she walked away. "Don't think it's going to be that kind of night."

When she went into Haley's bedroom, she found it quiet and empty. She stepped back out into the hallway, seeing a light on at the other end of the house. She walked back through, finding Haley out on the deck, still holding her wineglass from earlier.

She opened the door, then paused. "Want company?"

Haley turned and nodded. "Yes. Mike got settled?"

"He did. I think he's planning on sleeping with his weapon." She moved up next to her, stopping by the railing. "You want to talk?"

Haley let out a quiet breath. "I'm having a hard time seeing her." She turned slightly to look at her. "She used to be so crystal clear. I could see her face, her eyes, her expressions. This last year…it's been harder to see her." She took a swallow of the wine. "I think about being with you, you know. I've thought about it a lot, actually."

Carter nodded but said nothing.

"Truth is, I'm terrified of…of sleeping with you."

"Why is that?"

Haley put her wineglass on the railing and turned to her. "A couple of reasons, I guess. One, there's never been anyone but Gail. I'm thirty-three-freaking-years-old," she said, her voice breaking with emotion. "What if it's great?"

"What if it is?"

"Then…should it be? I mean—"

"Honey, Gail's been gone a long time."

"I know. I know. But then, I'm thinking, what if you chase her away? I mean, I can hardly see her anymore as it is. Then what will I have?"

Carter touched her face gently. "What do you have now?"

"I…I have memories," she said weakly. "I still have that." She wiped at a tear on her cheek.

"You'll always have memories, Haley. They might not be as fresh, as vibrant, but you'll always have memories." She moved closer. "She's gone, sweetie."

"I know. I just…I've been afraid to let her go."

Carter nodded. "Why don't I sleep on the sofa tonight. Let you—"

"No. I…I loved having you in bed last night. It was comforting and it felt…I don't know, it felt strange, but it felt good." She wiped at a tear. "I know I'm not making any sense." She attempted a smile. "I like you a lot, Carter. If I'm ever going to let someone take Gail away, maybe it should be you."

"I don't want to take her away from you. No one should take her away."

"I'm just so lonely," Haley said, her voice cracking with tears. "I've been able to fight it but you…you came in and…and flirted with me and I just…I didn't dismiss you like I normally do."

"Oh? Others have tried?" she asked with a smile.

"Yes," Haley said, smiling through her tears. "Yes, they have. I've not ever even considered it. And you, I don't know, I think I feel something with you. It scares the hell out of me, considering you're going to be leaving here in a little while."

"Let's just deal with today, hmmm?"

She cupped Haley's face with one hand, gently drawing her nearer. Haley didn't protest as she leaned closer. It was a slow, soft, almost quiet kiss. Quiet except for the tiniest of moans. When she pulled back, the shadows were too heavy to see Haley's eyes clearly, but she could feel her thundering heartbeat against her fingers.

"Okay?" she asked quietly. "Scary?"

"Yes. Scary. I feel fluttery in my stomach." Then Haley gave a short laugh. "Been years since I've felt that."

Carter smiled too. "Come on. Let's go to bed. Get some sleep."

"Sleep? Is that what you want? Was the kiss not okay for you?"

Carter smiled again. "It was very much okay. And when you're ready for more, we'll do more. There's no rush."

"So we'll go to sleep, and you'll hold me like last night?"

"Yes."

She leaned closer, intending to repeat the gentle kiss but Haley moved too, their bodies now touching. She was surprised when Haley's arms went around her neck but not so surprised that she didn't pull her closer. She didn't know which of them deepened the kiss, but she felt it down to her toes. Her moan matched Haley's when their mouths opened and their tongues met, shyly, then with more hunger.

Haley pulled away first, but she didn't move out of her arms. Her words were a bit breathless as she whispered into her ear.

"I don't want to just go to sleep. Okay?"

CHAPTER THIRTY-SEVEN

Haley clutched Carter's hand as they made their way through the house and to her bedroom. Her emotions were all over the place, and tiny voices were clamoring to be heard, so loud and jumbled that she heard none of them. No, all she heard was a rush in her ears from her rapidly beating heart. Was she really going to do this? There were times, in the early days, where she was certain that she'd never let another woman touch her. That part of her was reserved for Gail only. She'd felt nearly repulsed at the thought of being with someone else. As the years crawled by, nothing had changed in that regard.

Yet, here she was, feeling her pulse beating excitedly in a way it hadn't in so many years, she hardly recognized it. It was the kiss that had pushed her over. Not the first one. That one was sweet, hesitant, as if Carter were afraid she'd run. It was the second one, the one that sent a surge of arousal through her—a foreign concept, indeed—and made her knees feel weak. The one where Carter had pulled her close, where their mouths had opened to each other, where a tentative tongue had touched hers, making her moan. She knew then she didn't want a repeat of last night. She didn't want to simply crawl into bed with Carter and have her hold her.

No. She wanted to be touched. She wanted to feel alive. She wanted to feel passion and hunger and desire—all things she'd told herself she didn't need or want. Carter made her want them, though.

"Are you scared?"

She smiled at Carter's whispered words. "A lot of thoughts running through my mind, but surprisingly, that's not one of them." They were still holding hands and she brought Carter's up, placing it against her breast. She closed her eyes as Carter cupped her, feeling her nipple harden when Carter's finger brushed across it.

A warm mouth found hers then and she opened to it, letting Carter's tongue inside. Old feelings and new feelings seemed to mix, yet she knew it was Carter touching her, not Gail. Their clothes disappeared in a heap, landing together on the floor around them. She was the one to draw Carter into the bed, sighing with both relief and longing when Carter's body covered hers.

She couldn't even guess how she would feel in the morning, and she didn't want to. She would deal with her emotions then. Right now, she just wanted to enjoy this time with Carter without worrying about the consequences.

So she closed her mind and opened her heart, relishing the feeling of Carter's mouth moving against her skin, of warm lips covering her nipple, of soft, unfamiliar hands touching her in places no one else ever had...except Gail.

The tears came suddenly then, surprising her with their fierceness. Carter lifted her head, but Haley pulled her back down, holding her tightly.

"Don't stop. Please...don't stop."

"Haley—"

"I want this. I *need* this," she managed as she cried. "Please, Carter...make love to me. Chase it all away, please."

"Don't hate me."

"No. I need you."

Her tears still fell when Carter went back to her breast, when Carter's hands spread her thighs. They fell harder when Carter's fingers slipped into her wetness, brushing against her. It didn't feel foreign any longer. Carter's touch seemed familiar now, different as she recognized the subtle differences, yet familiar, as if Carter had touched her before.

Her tears seemed to fade away as her breath came in quick gasps, as her body trembled in anticipation. Carter's mouth came to hers again and she moaned into the kiss, arching off the bed, meeting Carter's fingers in a final push before she climaxed.

Carter held her tightly, brushing her lips across her face, whispering soothing words to her, words Haley didn't hear. With her eyes still closed, her body still throbbing, she could almost feel her broken heart trying to mend. It also wasn't lost on her the significance of it all. Today was the anniversary of Gail's death and another woman had made love to her.

She finally opened her eyes, reaching up a hand to brush at the hair on Carter's face. "Thank you."

Carter simply nodded, then lowered her head, kissing her so gently it made her smile. She brought Carter's mouth back to hers, deepening the kiss before rolling them over. She pulled back, trying to see Carter's eyes in the darkness.

"It's been forever since I've touched someone—since someone has touched me. I'd forgotten how it felt."

"You cried."

"Yes."

"I'm glad it was me."

"Me too." Haley lowered her head to kiss her. "I believe today is your birthday."

"I believe you're right."

"What shall we do to celebrate?"

"Well, off the top of my head, I can think of one thing," Carter teased.

"Yes. I can think of a couple too," she murmured before kissing her again.

Gone were her fears, her doubts. Gone was the uncertainty of how she'd react if she made love to someone—to Carter. She felt lighter, freer. She felt, in some ways, *younger*—like years had disappeared. Or perhaps she simply felt like herself again, before the weight of grief had nearly smothered her.

The feel of Carter's skin was so familiar to her, there was no hesitation in her touch. Her eyes closed as her mouth moved to Carter's breast and she let a contented moan escape as her lips closed around a nipple, her tongue rubbing across its surface.

Yes, she felt free. Finally.

CHAPTER THIRTY-EIGHT

Carter leaned against the counter, sipping on coffee as she watched Haley slice mushrooms. They'd gotten precious little sleep, yet she felt invigorated, rested. Content. And for some strange reason, Darla came to mind. An image of them in bed together, going through the motions of making love. She was never emotionally involved with Darla, she knew that. Darla wasn't invested in her either. The difference between being with Haley and being with Darla was glaring. Darla was someone to have sex with. Nothing more. Carter had found a softer, gentler side of herself with Haley.

"You're staring," Haley said without looking.

"Can't I stare?"

Haley glanced at her briefly, then went back to her mushrooms. "What are you thinking?"

Carter pushed off the counter, going closer. "I was thinking how much I loved kissing along the hollow of your back."

Haley's hands stilled, then she released the knife and turned to her. "I quite liked it, yes." Haley held her gaze and Carter could see the smile in her eyes. "I liked it when you kissed other places too."

Carter leaned closer, kissing her lightly, again feeling a sense of contentment wash over her. "We can maybe do that again tonight, hmm?"

Haley touched her face, drawing her closer for another kiss. "I feel good this morning, Carter. All the things I thought I'd feel—guilt, mainly, and maybe a sense of loss—I don't. I feel good. Normal. Dare I say happy? And that's certainly not anything I've felt in the last seven, eight years." Haley dropped her hand. "Thank you for that, Carter."

"You don't feel sad?"

Haley took a deep breath. "Sad? I don't even know what that word means anymore. Sad is how I would have described myself for all these years, but even then, it evolved. I evolved. You were right. Gail has been gone for a long time. Honestly, I don't know why I let it go on for as long as I did." She picked up the knife again. "Well, I do know. I was heartbroken and convinced that I would never heal. I guess I told myself that often enough and believed it to be true." She put the knife down once again and moved closer. "Thank you for last night, Carter. It was special. I feel like a new person really." Haley smiled as she touched her arm. "It might take me a while to get used to me." She leaned closer and kissed her. "And yes, maybe tonight we could—"

Haley stopped speaking when they heard the slamming of Mike's door. Carter picked up her cup and moved away, going to refill it.

"Can I help with something?"

"I'm making a ham and cheese frittata. Other than the mushrooms, I'll add a few onions to it. I thought we could go over the topo map while it baked. You still want to, right?"

"Yes. And I guess I should check my email in case Jason sent me something." She was adding sugar to her coffee when Mike stumbled in. "And good morning," she said brightly.

He muttered "Morning" as he moved past her to the coffeepot.

"How did you sleep?"

"I slept like crap. I woke up practically every hour, thinking someone was about to break in through the window."

"Yeah, well, when I checked on you earlier, you were snoring like you weren't worried about a thing."

He flicked his eyes at her. "I don't snore."

"Right." She put her cup down. "Gonna go get my laptop, see if Jason sent anything yet."

* * *

They had a large topo map spread out on the table and the three of them hovered over it. Jason was tweaking his program, he said, since it returned four probabilities, the two highest being the now-closed campgrounds. He hoped to have something before noon. In the meantime, they'd do it the old-fashioned way.

"This is the least used road," Haley said, pointing to Forest Road 709. She ran her finger along its path. "Definitely four-wheel-drive when you get past this cutoff."

"Where does the cutoff go?"

"There's a small stream back there. It's nice and flat. Tent campers like it. Lots of easy hiking. I've not driven the road past the cutoff, but I've hiked it. I would guess there were five or six side trails where people have made camps before."

"Might be a good one to check out," Mike said. "Little traffic."

"Where does the road go?" she asked.

"It loops around and hits up with Forest Road 708 which ends up back on Main Street. There's another—708A—that takes you way up above Timber Falls," Haley said. "Great views up there of the river and the town. There's not really any places to camp along that road. It's pretty much straight up until you get to the overlook at the top."

"Okay. What else? What about the other roads?"

"River Road becomes Forest Road 710 up past Sam's place," Mike said.

"Sam's River Runners," Haley supplied. She pointed to a spot on the map. "He's here. This is by far the longest road. It goes all the way around the peaks to the north and you can end up in Creede."

"Hell of a long ride, though," Mike added. "The road is not maintained. Never know what you might find. I'd guess less than ten Jeeps give it a try each summer. Take you most of the day to make the whole trip. Then you've still got to get back."

"Okay. So again, another road that doesn't have a lot of traffic."

"The first few miles of this road are pretty easy," Haley said. "You wouldn't need four-wheel drive until you got farther up. In case you don't think he has a vehicle like that."

"They haven't found where he purchased a vehicle, so my thought is that he stole one. Targeting a four-wheel-drive is going to be a little more complicated than a conventional car."

"Doesn't mean he had to steal it himself," Mike said. "Especially in Vegas. That'd mean he'd have to have enough cash, though. He worked maintenance, you said. Can't imagine that paid well."

"Reynolds's team is looking into his finances. I think we should go with the assumption that he has a four-wheel-drive." She tapped the map. "Let's start here with Forest Road 709."

"If you want to shower, there's about twenty more minutes on breakfast," Haley said.

"Okay, I think I will. Thanks." She met her gaze for a moment, smiling slightly. Haley's return smile was affectionate, she noticed, and she gave a quick nod before leaving. She wondered if Mike saw the look that passed between them.

* * *

As soon as Carter left the kitchen, Mike turned to her, his eyebrows raised questioningly. Haley ignored him, going instead to pull plates down, intending to set the table.

"Oh, come on. Don't I get anything?"

"I don't know what you're talking about."

He laughed. "The spare bedroom is not that far from yours, you know."

"Oh my god!" She whipped around, knowing her face had turned scarlet. "You couldn't possibly have heard anything."

He laughed again. "No. Not at all. But thanks for confirming. So how was it?"

She was about to tell him to mind his own business, but she didn't. She sat down at the table, facing him.

"It was wonderful, actually. Carter was so sweet. Even when I cried, she—"

"You cried?"

"I was a bit of an emotional wreck at first, yes. But I feel so good today, Mike. Like a weight has been lifted." She laughed a little. "Maybe I should have done this years ago."

"I told you to sleep with that girl who was working for you that one time."

"Girl being the key word there. She was nineteen, I think. Marlin. But I wasn't ready then, I guess. Carter, though, she... well, it was just so easy with her."

"Maybe it was easy because you genuinely like her."

"Yes, I do." She stood up, going to check the oven. "I'll miss her when she's gone. She's become someone I can talk to. I haven't had a female friend since Gail." She closed the oven door, thinking the frittata needed another ten minutes. "Nothing against you—because you know I love you to death— but it's been a welcome change to have her here."

"I'm going to miss her being around too. Someone my own age to grab a beer with, for one thing."

Haley nodded. "Yes, she fits in quite nicely at the bar, doesn't she?"

"Perfectly. Speaking of that, you're not rushing over there this morning. You trust CeCe by herself?"

"I doubt there's much of a rush, if any. If yesterday was any indication, the town will be deserted today. I guess I didn't realize how many people use those campgrounds."

"The RV campground is mostly older folks. They don't run the river. A few maybe. Most of them cook there too. I imagine all the eating places in town will be hurting."

"Yes. Let's hope it's over soon. There's still enough left of summer to make up for this lull."

Yes, she wanted it over with as soon as possible, of course she did. But that meant that Carter would be leaving town then. What would she be like after that, she wondered? Would she go back into her shell? Would she continue to live her life in the past, as if Gail might return to her? Wasn't that what Carter had said to her once? That she was waiting around for Gail—or her ghost—to visit? *Is* that what she'd been doing? To some extent, yes. Well, she didn't *really* think Gail would visit, not in that sense.

But isn't that why she'd come up here to Timber Falls—to feel close to Gail? Didn't she secretly hope that Gail would come to her in some way, hoping that she would feel her presence and be comforted by it?

That, of course, never happened. Yet she kept searching, didn't she? Kept holding out hope that one day she'd feel her. Did that mean that she'd now given up on that? Had she let all of that go? Had she given Gail enough years?

She absently twisted the wedding band on her finger, her gaze drawn to it. Had she? If so…then now what? Now what was she going to do?

CHAPTER THIRTY-NINE

Carter drove them up the bouncy, rocky road that wound through the trees, heading higher up the mountain above town. As had been the case each day, the sky was sunny and blue, a dark vibrant blue.

"Is it always like this?"

"What's that?"

"The weather."

"Except when it snows," Mike said dryly.

"I meant in the summer."

"Yeah, pretty much. Afternoon thunderstorms will start popping up before too long. At first, they're here then gone. Late July and August, they'll be a little more numerous. They don't disrupt the river too much, though. If it's a big lightning storm, they scramble to get the rafts out of the water 'til it passes, but that's about the extent of it."

"When does the snow start?"

"Up this high, we usually get a dusting in October, at least. Sometimes more. By December, there's usually snow on the ground and it's staying colder during the days. January and February are the coldest months but that's not to say there aren't some nice, sunny days." He smiled at her. "You like it up here, huh?"

"Yeah, I do."

"Does Haley have something to do with that?"

She glanced at him quickly, then looked back to the road. "What do you mean?"

"Oh, hell, Carter, it's not a secret what happened last night. Haley told me."

"She did? I figured she'd want to keep it a secret."

"Well, I dragged it out of her. About damn time she let go of that ghost."

"Don't know if that's what she did. I think maybe she just finally accepted that Gail is gone, and she still has a life to live." She slowed as they came to a fork in the road. "Is that the cutoff?"

"Yeah. Let's buzz down there real quick. Doubt our guy would camp there. As Haley said, it's mostly used by people who want to get some hiking in."

"No trail, though?"

"No. Most follow the little stream up and back. Easy hiking."

She could tell the cutoff road was used more frequently than the main road. They came to a clearing a short time later where the road ended. There were no vehicles parked there, but she saw evidence that someone had camped there. Rocks had been piled in circles for make-do campfire rings. Instead of stopping, she made the circle and headed back.

"You think this is a waste of time?" she asked Mike.

"If we think he's up here camping somewhere, then no. Without your guy Jason giving us somewhere concrete to look—and I don't know how that's even possible—all we can do is what we're doing. Still think we might have a better chance of finding him if we got the sheriff's department to help out."

"Murdock didn't think so and I tend to agree. If he's here hiding somewhere, then he's still on his mission. But if he senses that we're looking for him—and having a bunch of deputies driving official units around would do it—then he's likely to take off and disappear on us. Much better chance to find him on our own."

"Stumble upon him, you mean? Or do you think this Jason fella will pinpoint him for us?"

"Like you, I don't see how. Jason would have no way of knowing where these little spots are that people can camp. I think we'll be on our own."

She came back to the fork again and turned right, heading back up the mountain. They found a few pullouts and small clearings where people had camped before, but there was no sign of anyone about. It was another mile or two up the road before they saw signs of life. A blue tent was nestled in the trees, but there was no vehicle around.

She pulled off the road and onto the little lane that ended under the trees. "What do you think?"

"We can snoop around a bit, I guess."

The wind was a little stronger up that high, and she knew why the tent had been erected among the trees, giving it some protection. It was zippered up and she hesitated only a moment before bending down to find the zipper and open the door. The inside was neat and tidy. One sleeping bag, a small pillow, and a duffel bag of clothes was all that was there. She closed it again, then stood, looking around.

Mike lifted the lid on a white cooler and peered inside. "Got beer, some cheese, an opened package of wieners, and some turkey slices." He looked at her. "The ice hasn't melted yet. Might only be a day old."

She looked around the campsite, finding tire treads. She walked around, following them. "They go up, not down." She gazed back from where they'd come. "Look at this view. Anyone camping here has a view of the road. If it's our guy, he could have seen us driving up and took off." She pointed up the mountain. "Where does this road go again?"

"It loops around the back side of the mountain and hits 708."

"And 708 is Main Street?"

"Yeah. Well, technically the highway comes into town, turns into Main Street, and simply ends. The forest road just dumps onto the end of Main."

"Okay. And there's a 708A somewhere too?"

"That's the one that goes above the falls."

She nodded. "Then let's keep going."

It took them nearly two hours to drive the whole loop and she was glad she'd rented a four-wheel-drive SUV. Even then, they'd had to crawl over rocks and through ruts. It was slow-going and she felt that time was slipping away from them. They came upon only one other campsite, this one with two tents. There were four guys there, all college students who had been run off from the campground down below. They were staying through tomorrow, taking a chance to run the river one more time, they said. And no, they hadn't seen another vehicle come down the mountain.

When they made it back into town, it was indeed deserted. No cars traveled down Main, no people lingered along the sidewalks, staring into shop windows.

"Well, goddamn," Mike murmured. "It's worse than a winter day." He pointed to a side lane. "Let's go check out the lodge."

She turned where he'd indicated. "What about the motel?"

"Yeah, it's down on the corner. Not much to it—twenty-something rooms is all, but they stay booked all summer. Now the lodge, that's more high-end, a little fancier. Some of those rooms have kitchenettes too. That's the pecking order in town—the lodge, then the motel, then the RV campground, then the tent campgrounds."

"And they all stay booked?"

"Oh, there'll be some instances during the week where you might could find a camping site, but the rooms are all booked."

There were only a handful of vehicles at the lodge, even fewer at the motel. "You'd think they would feel safer in a room with a locked door," she said.

"Most everybody comes to town to run the river at some point. So even though they may be staying in a room and not a tent, having two young men—who had also come here to run the river—get brutally murdered most likely spooked them all."

"I know even a few days like this will really hurt the businesses in town, but I'm glad most everyone left. Makes it easier to find this guy."

"Yeah, we had so much luck this morning."

"So let's take another road. Where to?"

"Let's head up 710."

"That's the one that crosses over to...what did you say? Creede?"

"Yeah. We'll go on up a few miles, maybe ten or so. Ten miles on a bouncy dirt road will take a good hour. Can't see our guy making a camp that far from town. Can you?"

"Probably not."

CHAPTER FORTY

Besides Scott, Charlie, and Bill, Haley had only four other customers for lunch and all four of them were heading out of town after doing one last short run that morning.

"This reminds me of back in the early days," Charlie said. "Weren't hardly nobody in town back then. Of course, weren't no shops neither."

"It'll pass," Scott said.

"I heard from Randy over at the lodge that he's got people canceling rooms for next week too," Bill chimed in.

"That ain't good," Charlie said. "The town better hope Mike and that FBI gal can put an end to this madness real quick like. Next thing you know, Timber Falls will be a *real* ghost town."

They all laughed nervously, then Scott said, "That won't happen."

Haley moved away as they argued among themselves, absently wiping down the bar as she went. She'd sent Sylvia home and Rhonda too. So far, her seasonals hadn't mentioned leaving. According to CeCe, they all felt safe having rooms upstairs. She did notice that most of them were still hanging out at the saloon and not on the river today.

She looked up as the bell jingled, smiling as Mike came in. She automatically glanced behind him, disappointed that Carter wasn't with him.

"She's on the phone," Mike said, reading her thoughts. "Reynolds again."

"Any luck?" she asked as she drew him a beer.

"Yeah, you find anything?" Charlie asked from down at the end.

Mike held his hand up to ward off any other questions. "No updates to give, fellas. But when I do know something, you three will be the very first to know."

Charlie mumbled something under his breath, and Haley gave Mike a wink as she brought him a beer.

"I guess that means you didn't stumble upon him?"

"No. Found an unoccupied campsite. Drove back up there again, but still no one was there. Carter has some crazy plan about sneaking up after midnight to see if there's a vehicle."

"So you've been driving all day?"

"Yep. Taking the time to show Carter the scenery. We even drove up to the overlook above the falls. I think she's taken with the place. She'll miss it here when she's gone."

"She's only been around a week or so. I feel like I've known her much longer."

Mike took a big swallow of his beer, nodded. "Yeah, she's easy." He turned slightly, giving them a little more privacy from the guys. "Lab called while we were out. It's for sure this Dickenson fella. Weren't any prints in the Jeep, but it was his DNA under the nails of young Trevor Greene."

"And you don't remember him?" she asked quietly.

"I remember the case a little but mostly from reading that file Jason sent her. Without that jogging my memory, if I ran into the guy, I wouldn't have remembered him." Then he grinned. "And him dressed like a woman don't hardly count."

Haley patted his hand. "Well, I have faith that you two will find him. Because if you don't, you'll both probably be run out of town."

"Yeah, I know. Sam called me again today, telling me how many thousands of dollars he's losing." He glanced around at the empty dining room. "I know you're hurting too."

"Not as bad as the Raft House, apparently. Bill heard they shut down early yesterday, because there was no dinner crowd and nothing for breakfast either."

"I don't know why they open for breakfast at all. You and Flip got that market covered."

"Well, there wasn't exactly a rush on breakfast today, that's for sure." The bell jingled and she glanced up, conscious of the smile on her face as Carter came in. Carter met her gaze, smiling at her before sitting down beside Mike.

"I'll have one of those," she said, motioning to Mike's beer. "Been a long day."

Mike nudged her. "What did you learn?"

"Found out why Dickenson has a penchant for cutting off penises." Carter picked up the beer Haley placed there. "Thanks."

"Prison?" Mike guessed.

"Oh, yeah. He was being raped repeatedly by his cellmate. They wouldn't move him. Apparently, child abusers and the like aren't well received. But there's records of it. His attorney filed complaints and threatened legal action. It drug out for months. Don't know how Dickenson got a knife in the cell, but one night, he cut off the guy's penis."

"Jesus Christ," Mike whispered. "Killed him?"

"No, but the guy probably wished he had."

"I'm surprised Dickenson got released then."

"They deemed it self-defense."

"In other words, they brushed it under the rug because they wouldn't move the guy." Mike shook his head. "You almost feel for him. Hell, he's in prison for a crime he didn't commit, he's getting raped because of that crime, I'd probably snap too."

"There's a lot of innocent people in this, but he's not one of them," Carter said. "Not any longer."

"I know. But just think how many lives are affected because I arrested him."

"You did your job," Carter said.

"Neither of you have told me the whole story about this guy. Why do you say he was innocent?"

"I arrested him for killing his kid. The way it looks, the wife did it, not him."

"They couldn't prove either of them, so they were both convicted of a lesser crime," Carter explained. "He maintained his innocence throughout."

"Thus the revenge he's after," Haley stated.

"Right. Killed the wife. Killed the prosecutor. I'm next," Mike said.

She leaned closer to Carter. "You think he's still around Timber Falls?"

"I do. We found one suspicious site."

She nodded. "Mike says you want to go in after midnight."

"I do."

"You better get to bed early then," she said with a wink. A blush lit Carter's face, causing her to laugh. "Really? You can still blush?"

"Oh, you two, please," Mike muttered with a roll of his eyes.

CHAPTER FORTY-ONE

"Tell me about your childhood."

Carter rolled onto her back, wondering where that question had come from. Haley turned too, resting on her side. Carter's eyes closed as Haley's fingers brushed across her stomach.

"Tell me about yours," she countered.

"Okay," Haley said easily. "I'm the only child. Now that I think about it, I was pretty lonely growing up too. My parents are older." She paused only slightly. "I was adopted. They were almost forty at the time. Well, my dad was over forty. My mom thirty-eight. Their siblings all had children much younger in life, so by the time I was old enough to run around and remember family gatherings, I was the only kid there, really."

"Are you close with them?"

"My parents or the family?"

"Both."

"My parents and I have a normal relationship, I guess. As soon as I was old enough to understand, they let me know that I had been adopted. I think they were afraid one of my cousins would say something." Haley's hand slipped lower, caressing her hip. "I'm not close to any of them, no. The one closest to my age is twelve years older." She paused again, letting out a heavy breath. "After Gail's accident, as you know, I kinda ran away. My grandmother lent me the money for the saloon. My parents weren't exactly happy with her."

"So you're close to her then?"

"I was, yes. She died the year after I moved here. That was another contentious thing—the money. She had two other children besides my mother. They knew she'd given me the money. I was to pay it back a little each month. That was our agreement. I had no idea, but she'd had papers drawn up with her attorney, not only forgiving the loan but also leaving me a portion of her estate."

"That didn't go over too well, I take it."

"Not at all. To this day, there's still a rift between my mother and them. I haven't seen or talked to anyone in my family since the funeral. Well, other than my parents, of course. We talk often and they've been out to visit three or four times, I guess." Haley's hand slid up to her breast. "So that's me. Now what about you?"

She closed her eyes as fingers brushed against her nipple. "I already told you."

"You were the forgotten middle child. How does that happen?"

"Didn't I say? I was a surprise pregnancy that they didn't want. They also couldn't go through with the abortion."

Haley's hand stilled. "What do you mean?"

"My mother had a change of heart while she was on the table. Reggie used to tease me that I'd been *this close*."

"Oh my god. How did you find this out?"

She swallowed, remembering the look in her mother's eyes. "I think I was thirteen. My mother and I were having an argument about something, and she threw one of my schoolbooks across the room. She told me she wished she'd gone through with the abortion after all because I was the only one who caused her misery."

"You have got to be kidding."

"Oh, when she realized what she'd said, she tried to make light of it. But I understood then what the pecking order was in the family and that I was definitely one notch below the dog."

"Oh, sweetie, that's awful."

"I turned out okay, I guess."

"Yes, you did. No wonder you don't have a relationship with them."

"I think it's one reason I poured myself into the job. Once you make detective, you can pretty much work 24/7 and that's what I did for the most part. There wasn't a lot of idle time."

"No time to think?"

She rolled to her side, facing Haley. "Not so much that. I didn't give them much thought really. Every eight months to a year, I'd hear from my mother or my sister. The conversations were usually short and one-sided." She leaned closer, kissing her, wanting to change the subject. "I should really get some sleep, but having you naked beside me makes me want to do something other than sleep."

She felt Haley smile against her lips. "Instead of getting up at midnight, why don't you stretch it to one or two and we *can* do something other than sleep."

"Mike thinks we should go about three anyway."

"Oh, now you tell me. I would have drawn it out earlier then."

Carter laughed lightly. "I think you drew it out long enough." She felt Haley move closer, and she pressed against her. "Are you okay with everything?"

"Everything? You mean you in my bed, naked?"

"Yeah. That."

"I don't feel guilty or anything like that if that's what you're asking. I won't lie. I think about her. When you touch me, I think about her, try to remember her that way. It's been too long, I guess. When you kiss me, I don't feel her kisses—it's just you. I don't even remember what they were like."

"I was afraid…well, I was afraid you wanted me to be a fill-in for her. A nameless, faceless body that you could pretend was Gail."

"If that's all I wanted, I would have found someone years ago." Haley pushed her to her back and rested her weight on top. "I needed this, Carter. I needed someone to make me let her go. Why you? Why now? I don't really know. And I don't guess it matters."

The kiss Haley gave her then signaled they were through talking. She reversed their positions, spreading Haley's thighs and settling between them.

CHAPTER FORTY-TWO

"I'd kill the lights," Mike said quietly, as if someone would hear him inside her vehicle.

"How do you propose I see to drive then?"

"I'm guessing we're about a mile away. Let's go up on foot."

Carter shook her head. "I don't like that idea. Let's drive right up to the campsite. If someone's there, we confront them. If it's not him, we say sorry and go on."

"And hope no one comes out of the tent with a gun?"

"We're both armed. I think we can handle it."

She drove slowly, and it seemed to take an eternity to reach the last curve before the campsite. The anticipation she'd felt vanished though. There was no vehicle there.

"That's odd," Mike whispered.

"Let's take a look." They both had flashlights out and to be safe, she flashed the light on the tent. "Anybody home?" she called loudly.

It was eerily quiet. If not for the breeze rustling the trees, she would say it was deathly quiet.

"That food cooler is still here," Mike said. He lifted the lid and peered inside. "Ice is melting. Looks like someone's been here, though. The wieners are gone."

She went to the tent and unzipped the door. The inside wasn't neat as it had been. The sleeping bag was rumpled, like someone had used it.

"Maybe he saw us and took off up the mountain," Mike suggested from behind her.

"We would have seen his lights. Besides, it's three in the morning. If someone was here, they'd be sleeping." She zipped the tent up again. "You can't see shit without lights. No moon. If he took off in his car, he'd likely drive off the side of the mountain."

"So now what?"

* * *

Haley took her coffee out to the deck—her coffee and the cozy throw blanket she often used. She'd tried to go back to sleep when they'd left, but it eluded her. She sat down in her usual chair and looked up into the sky. There was no moon that she could see, and she supposed it had already set. The stars were bright, and she stared at them, her gaze moving from one to another absently.

She was aware of how blissfully relaxed she felt. She didn't know if it was physical—having had sex—or mental. Maybe a little of both. She smiled in the darkness, feeling happy and content, something she hadn't felt in a very long time. Carter was the one on her mind, not Gail. And that was okay. There was no guilt, for that she was thankful. Gail's accident had shaken her to her core and had taken nearly eight years of her life. If Carter hadn't walked in, she wondered how many more years Gail would have taken from her.

Oh, that wasn't really fair, was it? Gail hadn't taken those years. No, Haley had simply given them to her willingly. Her heart was broken, never to mend.

Until it did, seemingly overnight.

Yes. She smiled again as she took a sip of her coffee. She felt healed. She felt whole again. She felt like herself again. Alive. Carter made her feel alive. Carter made her feel a lot of things. She—

A flash of headlights through the trees made her draw her brows together. The small lane that went past Mike's house to hers, then on up to where Tim and Sarah Randall lived— they owned one of the shops in town—never had traffic of any sort. Besides, it was four in the morning. Who would be out at that hour? Surely Carter and Mike weren't back already. She stood and went to the railing, but the lights turned off as she watched. She listened, hearing the low rumble of a car's engine. It appeared to be down at the very end of her long driveway.

Just as panic was about to set in, the lights came back on. She could tell the car was backing up onto the road again, then it turned, heading toward town. Without thinking, she hurried inside, pausing to lock the door behind her. She put her cup down, then nearly ran to her bedroom, finding her phone. Carter answered right away.

"Hey. Shouldn't you be in bed?"

"Couldn't sleep." She paused, wondering if she was overreacting. "There was a car here."

"What? When?"

"Just now. I was out on the deck. I saw the headlights. They parked at the end of the driveway, killed the lights for a few seconds, then they left."

"Are you sure they left? Are the doors locked?"

"Yes to both."

"Okay. We're on our way back, almost to town already. There was nothing up there. But Haley, turn on all your lights, porch lights, everything. Mike says we're about ten minutes from you. I'll make it in five."

She walked around, turning on lights as she went. At the front door, she flipped on the outside porch light, then jerked the blinds closed on the side window.

"Told her years ago she needed a gun," she heard Mike say.

"He told me that when the bear chased me. I don't think he meant as protection from a killer."

"A bear chased you?"

She stood in the hallway, away from any windows. "Yes. On a hike. She had two cubs." She was thankful Carter was staying on the phone with her. "Where are you now?"

"Just passing the saloon."

"Christ, Carter, will you slow down," Mike said.

Haley felt relieved that Carter was racing toward her. Still, she eyed the hall closet. Should she hide? Was she in any danger?

"Do you see lights anywhere?"

Haley frowned. "Me?"

"No, Mike. Thought maybe we might come upon whoever was at your house."

She couldn't make out what Mike said.

"Okay, we're turning onto your road. Coming up on Mike's place."

She realized she was holding her breath and she made herself relax. They were almost there.

"Okay, we're at your driveway. It's all quiet here."

"Good. I'm sorry, I panicked a little."

"You didn't sound panicked to me."

"Thank you, but I was," she said as she walked to the front door and unlocked it. When she opened it, she was still holding her phone to her ear as was Carter. They smiled at each other. "Hi."

"Hey." Carter pocketed her phone. "There was no sign of anyone driving around town. It was dark and quiet."

Mike came in behind her. "Any coffee left?"

Haley nodded and motioned to the kitchen, her eyes never leaving Carter's. "Help yourself."

CHAPTER FORTY-THREE

"Jason says Forest Road 709 has the highest probability," Carter said as she read through his email on her phone.

"No shit," Mike said dryly. "Don't need a damn computer to tell us that."

Carter flicked her eyes at him. "My gut says the abandoned campsite is his."

"The wieners were gone," Mike reminded her. "Not abandoned."

They were sitting at the bar in the saloon. Haley had sent CeCe back to bed, saying she would cover. Not that anyone expected a breakfast crowd. She smelled bacon frying now and her stomach rumbled. Haley was making them a "hearty breakfast" before they went out again. Seeing as how all three of them had been up since two that morning, existing on nothing but the caffeine in their coffees, she was ready for a hearty meal.

"What do you think this guy has been doing? I mean if he's been up here over a week, what's he been doing?"

"You mean besides killing?"

"Yeah. Has he run the river? Has he been doing surveillance? Has he been driving around, finding all his escape routes?"

"Run the river? You think he's that crazy?"

"What's crazy about it?" She picked up her coffee cup. The swallow she took was cool, and she pushed the cup away. "That would be a good way to get a feel for the place, maybe meet some of these young college kids, learn their routines. How else would he know that they normally stay up past midnight drinking?"

Mike shook his head. "They're college kids. Of course they're going to be up drinking."

"But only a section of them. A lot of the people who come up here are serious about the river. They go to bed early, get up early. Both of the guys who were killed were in this party section, right?"

"Yeah, I see what you mean. Unless this guy was familiar with the campground setup, he wouldn't know which part they were camping in."

"So let's run by Sam's. He has some sort of a ledger or something, doesn't he?"

"Oh, yeah. He gets all kinds of information from them. You know, in case someone drowns or something."

She looked out the window. It was fully daylight but still early. "You think he's keeping normal hours?"

"They start work at daybreak, getting all the rafts ready to roll. I imagine he's already there, customers or not. Routine."

"Then after we eat, let's go see him."

* * *

Haley stood in the doorway, watching Carter and Mike. They were so familiar with each other, like old friends. Yes, no doubt Mike would miss Carter too when she left. She wasn't ready to think about that, though. Carter looked up as if she felt her eyes on her. They smiled at each other as if they were the only two in the room. Mike nudged Carter, breaking the spell. Oh, yes, she would miss her.

With a sigh, she went back into the kitchen, just in time to flip the toast before they burned. She filled three plates, all with scrambled eggs, bacon and sausage both, a mound of hash browns, and the thick, buttered toast. She'd been ravenous when she'd started cooking, but now the mounds of food looked a bit much. With a skill she hadn't possessed a month ago, she carried the three plates at once out to the bar.

"Oh my god, that looks great," Carter exclaimed as she snatched a strip of bacon off hers before Haley had even put it down.

"Hungry?"

"Past that," Carter said. "Thank you."

Haley walked around the bar, sitting down next to Carter. "Do we have a plan?"

"Sort of. Gonna start with Sam," Carter said around a forkful of eggs.

"Why there?"

"Carter thinks our guy might have been running the river." She cut the sausage patty in half, then cut that portion too. "Seriously? Like he's on vacation or something?"

"More like getting the lay of the land," Carter said. "I can't decide if I like the sausage or the bacon best." She took a huge bite of the buttered toast. "But I definitely like this."

"Thank you. Other than a taco, I think it's the first real breakfast I've cooked for you. Well, other than the frittata."

"That's because I usually do the cooking."

"Yes, you do. And you're very good at it."

Carter laughed. "Cheap labor."

"It's a cushy job. You're sleeping with the boss."

Carter met her gaze, her expression softening. "Fringe benefits, huh?"

"Will you two stop? Can't even enjoy my breakfast with all this flirting going on."

Haley leaned forward, looking past Carter to Mike. "At least I didn't fall for a guy dressed as a woman."

Carter laughed. "She got you there, Mike."

Mike pointed his fork at them. "That little bit of information better not *ever* get out," he threatened.

They finished their breakfast in near silence, and she could tell both Mike and Carter were anxious to get going. When Carter put her fork down, signaling she was finished, Mike stole the remaining piece of bacon from her plate.

"Who knows when we'll eat again," he said as he chewed.

"I'm stuffed," Carter said. "That was excellent."

"Thanks."

"I'd stay to help clean up, but—"

"I know you need to go." She started to collect their plates, but Carter stopped her.

"A quick chat? In your office?"

"Come on, guys. Kiss goodbye and let's go."

Carter ignored him and tugged her along to the office anyway. She closed the door, then held her against it, bending close to kiss her.

"I kinda like you."

Haley smiled. "I kinda like you too." Her smiled faltered a little. "You're close to catching this guy?"

"I hope so. If that was him at your house this morning, then he's getting bold. I think he's ready for it to be over with too."

"Meaning Mike? Try to...kill him?"

"Yeah. I think he's through playing games. His attempt to frame Mike didn't work so he'll probably try to take him out. I would guess he's a little out of his mind by now. He wasn't a killer when he went to prison. It's assumed he's killed five people now. Don't know about his wife and the prosecutor, but those three young men were butchered."

"Out of his mind, meaning he's lost his sanity?"

"Yeah. He'll make poor decisions, like driving around this morning, looking for Mike. Assuming it was him and all."

Haley nodded, then separated from her. "So you might even find him today then."

"I hope so."

"Well, I certainly do too, but then that means you'll be leaving."

Their eyes held and Carter nodded slowly. "Yeah, it does."

"I don't know that I'm ready for that."

"Yeah, me either." Carter pulled her into a hug. "I need to go."

"Yes, I know. Please be careful."

Carter kissed her again, a sweet, lingering kiss that made her sigh with contentment. Their eyes held for a long moment afterward, then she nodded, releasing Carter.

Mike was leaning on the bar, his foot tapping impatiently. "Took you long enough."

"Not nearly long enough, trust me," Carter said. "You ready?"

"Been ready."

Carter turned to her. "You'll be okay here?"

Haley nodded. "Everyone is upstairs still. And Sylvia is due in at ten." She looked around the empty dining room. "Unless I call her to cancel her shift. I doubt we'll have a rush."

She'd no sooner said that when the bell jingled. All three of them turned to the door, seeing two young women come in. She smiled at them.

"Take any table you like. Coffee?"

"Yes, thanks."

Carter touched her arm as she passed. "Talk to you later."

Haley stared after them. "Be careful."

She watched Carter through the glass, then turned her attention to the young women who had come in. They were in their early twenties, she guessed. By their demeanor and the looks they shared, they were definitely a couple. It brought back memories of her and Gail at that age. She realized it was with fondness that she recalled that early time in her life. Fondness, yes. Not pain.

She grabbed the pot of coffee and went over to their table. "Good morning, ladies."

"Good morning," one said. "The town is kinda quiet, isn't it?"

"Yes, it is. When did you get here?'

"Yesterday."

"You staying at the lodge?"

"Yes. We didn't know there'd been a murder up here. We just found out when we got here."

"Yes, it's terrible. Nothing like that has ever happened here before. It kinda ran everybody off." She poured coffee into their cups. "Well, when they closed the campgrounds, everyone had to leave."

"Do you think it's safe here?"

"You mean on the river?" She smiled at them and nodded. "I think you'll be perfectly fine."

CHAPTER FORTY-FOUR

"When do they make the first run?" Sam's parking lot was all but vacant—four vehicles were parked there.

"Usually around eight," Mike said. "I'd guess the river will be plenty empty today."

She hadn't met Sam before and didn't know what to expect. He was a giant of a man with bushy eyebrows and a full beard. He shook her hand firmly.

"I hope you catch this bastard soon because he's likely to put me out of business."

"Well, we're hoping you might be able to help us."

"We want to take a look at your register," Mike explained.

"Especially license plates. You collect that info, right?" she asked.

"I do. What are we looking for?"

"Nevada plates, to start. Can we go back a week?"

"Sure. Come on back to my office."

His office was small and cluttered, but Carter didn't imagine you could get a better view than this. The river was practically right outside his window with the rock face of a mountain beyond that.

"Nice."

"Yeah, can't complain," he said as he sat down behind his desk. A few clicks and keystrokes later, he spun his monitor around. "This is pretty straightforward. These are yesterday's bookings. As you can see, we weren't overrun with customers."

She scanned the list, surprised to find a Nevada vehicle. She jotted down the plate number. "How do I look at previous days?"

"Use the dropdown menu. We keep a week's worth on the log, then archive it."

The days prior had four or five times the number of customers listed. No wonder he was concerned with the campgrounds closing. Mike peered over her shoulder, and they went through four days. There were only five vehicles with Nevada plates.

"I'll call Jewell and get her to run them," Mike said. He took the piece of paper with him and left the office.

Sam spun the monitor back around, pulling up yesterday's activity. "Had somebody from Nevada yesterday. This one here," he said, pointing to the name Richard Amber. "He didn't run the river. He rented a kayak, and the son of a bitch didn't bring it back."

"Where did he put in? Here?"

"No. They said he went upstream to the base of the falls then rode it down past town. Took out just before Dead Man Falls."

"You remember him?"

"Hell, yeah. I only had ten customers or so. Besides, I keep their driver's license when they rent stuff."

She took out her phone, swiping through the images until she came to the most recent photo they had of Edward Dickenson. She held it up and Sam nodded immediately.

"That's the bastard who stole my kayak."

"Can I see his driver's license?"

"Sure. It's out front." He stood and came around his desk, motioning her to follow.

Mike was coming back in when they walked back to the front. "The older model Jeep Cherokee was reported stolen. Vegas."

"Sam ID'd him. He rented a kayak yesterday. He's got to be our guy."

Sam's eyes widened. "You mean, the...the killer? That was him? Jesus Christ."

"Let me see his license," she said. "Name on the ledger is Richard Amber," she told Mike.

She and Mike both stared at the picture on the license, nodding. "That's him," they said in unison.

"Thanks, Sam. I'm going to keep this," she said, holding up the license.

"Okay, sure. You don't think he's coming back here, right?"

"If you see this guy, you call me," Mike said.

"As you know, I've got a shotgun behind the counter here. Killer or not, I ain't scared of him."

Mike shook his head. "Call me," he said as they walked outside. "What's the plan?" he asked when they were alone.

"Call the sheriff's department. See if they'll send a couple of units up here. We need more than you and me searching for this guy." She pointed to Sam's. "Probably wouldn't hurt to have someone parked here too."

"We going to drive up and check out the campsite again?"

Carter nodded. "Yeah. I don't know how I know—just a gut feeling—but I'm certain that's his camp."

CHAPTER FORTY-FIVE

They bounced up the mountain road, a road she was beginning to know the nuances of by now. She felt like she'd driven up the thing a dozen times or more. But they were getting close to him. She could feel it.

"That last switchback—if he's outside, he's got a view of the road," Mike reminded her.

"We'll have a view of his site too. Or at least we should be able to tell if a vehicle is there. The Jeep Cherokee we're looking for—what color is it?"

"Dark gray."

"Can you reach my pack there in the back seat? My binoculars are in there."

Mike took his seat belt off and shifted, only to bounce up and hit his head when her front tire fell into a hole.

"Goddamn, Carter," he muttered as he rubbed his head.

"Sorry."

They were getting close to the last curve, and she slowed. There were pockets of thick trees, then more open spaces where rock outcroppings replaced the trees. She slowed to a crawl as they approached the opening. Mike was leaning forward, binoculars to his face.

"Just a little farther," he said quietly. Then she felt him stiffen. "The bastard is there!"

"Same vehicle?"

"Yeah. Let's go!"

She pressed the gas pedal, tossing them both back against the seat as she took off as fast as the road—and her rented SUV—would allow. They were in the trees again and she could no longer see his campsite. When they came out into a clearing, she saw the Jeep Cherokee speeding up the mountain.

"Son of a bitch!"

She drove as fast as she dared and even then, they were getting beat to hell. She had a death grip on the steering wheel and Mike was holding onto the dash with one hand and the grab handle above the door with the other.

"I should have let you drive."

"You're doing fine, but I don't mind saying my Jeep would handle this road a little better."

He was far enough ahead of them that he disappeared around a corner just as they passed his campsite. She sped on, following him up the mountain road. When they rounded the corner, he was nowhere in sight.

"Keep going," Mike said. "There's no place for him to pull over and hide his vehicle."

She did and when they came into a clearing, they spotted him up ahead. It was a brief sighting as he disappeared once again. She continued on, watching as the Jeep came into view then gone again. When they rounded a bend in the road, she slammed on her brakes. The Jeep Cherokee was stopped, the door open.

"What do you think?"

Mike took her binoculars and scanned the area around the Jeep. "There!" He pointed. "He's on foot."

They got out, and she saw the white of his T-shirt through the trees. "What in the hell is he doing?"

"Looks like he's heading down to the river."

"From up here?"

"Listen. You can hear the falls."

She tilted her head, listening, hearing the roar of water off in the distance.

"I'm guessing he's climbing down to the base of the falls."

"You think he's got the kayak stashed there?" she asked as she ran after him.

"Maybe." Mike huffed beside her, keeping pace.

Into the trees they went, then she skidded to a halt, her eyes wide. "Christ, it's like straight down into the canyon."

"There he is!"

"Oh my god," she murmured. How the hell were they going to follow him? She'd fall for sure. She grabbed Mike's arm and met his gaze. "Okay. I'm going after him. You—"

"Hell, Carter, you're not a goddamned mountain goat. You can't—"

"If he can, I can. You take my car and go back down to the falls."

He shook his head. "The road doesn't go to the falls. It curves away just past Sam's place, where they put in. You can't drive to the falls."

"Shit. Okay, go back down to Sam's. If our guy is getting in the river, then he'll have to pass you there. Call the sheriff's deputies and see if they made it up here yet. Get them out looking for this guy too."

"Let me go after him. You go down and—"

"No. I don't know my way around here well enough. I don't know the deputies. Now go!"

"Okay, but Jesus Christ, Carter, don't do anything stupid."

"Yeah. Stupid like fall?"

"Yeah. That."

Their eyes held for a moment, then he nodded and took off back toward her car. He called over his shoulder to her. "Call me when you get a visual on him. He'll most likely get to the river before you catch up to him."

"If he gets in the river, you better damn well stop him," she yelled back as she took her first step down the mountain.

A loose rock had her grasping at a tree limb to keep from falling. "Not your best plan, Carter," she muttered as she righted herself.

The going was slow, and she knew he would be at the river long before she was. Even if he had the kayak hidden there, what was his plan? Ride the river as far as he could? From Mike's and Haley's descriptions of the river, she doubted a kayak would make it through Dead Man Falls. But if he did make it, then what? Head to the woods again? Did he have another vehicle stashed somewhere? Shouldn't matter. If he got in the river, Mike would get him. Provided he made it back down in time.

She lost her footing again, this time slipping down and banging her knee on the rocks. She looked down below her, seeing him a hundred feet or so ahead of her. As she watched, he turned. They stared at each other for a long moment, then he raised his hand. She ducked behind a rock a second before he shot at her. She saw the dirt kick up two feet away. She pulled her own weapon out. She didn't have a clear line of sight, but she fired twice as she scooted down toward him. He fired back, causing her to duck again.

"Bastard."

She looked around, trying to find the safest route down, one that would provide her some cover. A few more feet—ten or twelve—and she'd be out in the open. Beyond that, she'd be scrambling to get back into the trees again. She took a deep breath, counting silently to three before heading down again.

CHAPTER FORTY-SIX

Haley was pacing behind the bar, wishing like hell that Mike or Carter would call her. She knew something was going on. She'd seen three sheriff's department cars buzz by earlier and not fifteen minutes ago, she'd seen Carter's SUV speed past, heading up River Road. It was Carter's SUV, but Mike had been driving. There was no sign of Carter.

She was staring out the windows when Butter Bill came up the steps. She glanced at the clock on the wall, surprised that it was nearing the lunch hour. She hadn't had a single customer since 9:30 that morning.

She gave Bill a smile, knowing how forced it was. "Hey."

He nodded at her. "I went by Flip's this morning. The place was as empty as this."

"Yes. It's been quiet all morning," she said as she pulled a mug out for him.

"Heard there was some shooting going on."

She drew her brows together. "Shooting? Where?"

"In the canyon, up near the falls."

She placed the beer in front of him. "Does anybody know what it is?"

"Don't think so, but I saw that those deputies were in town. Something's going on."

"Yes, I saw them too."

He took a big swallow of his beer. "Heard from Sam that the killer was at his place yesterday."

"*What?*"

"Yeah. Said he rented a kayak. Of course Sam didn't know it was the killer at the time." He took another swallow. "Stole the kayak, he said. Never brought it back. Can't imagine he'd be so bold as to come out and rent a kayak. Can you?"

"That's because he probably didn't know that they'd ID'd him."

"They have? Well, who the hell is he?"

She shook her head quickly. "I don't know, really. They found some DNA or something," she said evasively.

They both turned when the door burst open. It was Charlie.

"Something's going on up at Sam's place," he said, his breathing labored as if he'd been running. "Heard from Delvin over at the grocery store that there were deputies in town again. You think there's been another killing?"

"I think maybe they got this guy cornered or something. Haley here says that they ID'd the killer."

"Who is it?" Charlie asked.

Haley held a hand up. "I don't know, but what's going on at Sam's?"

"Heard Mike was there with a couple of deputies," he said.

"I heard there was shooting up at the falls," Bill said.

"Shooting?"

A squealing of tires outside had them all turning to stare out the windows. A sheriff's department vehicle sped past, going downriver, not up.

"Wonder what the hell's going on," Charlie said.

Haley couldn't stand it any longer. "Sylvia is in the kitchen. Let her know if you want lunch. And Charlie, help yourself to a beer."

"Where are you going?" Bill asked.

"I'm going to Sam's."

"What the hell for? There's shooting going on out there! You best stay here with us, young Haley," Charlie said.

"No. I'm too worried to stay."

CHAPTER FORTY-SEVEN

Carter scrambled behind the trunk of a tree that was growing precariously at the edge of a drop-off. His shot slammed into the bark, splintering it. She reached around the tree blindly, firing in his direction. He was close to the river now, maybe only fifty feet away. She wouldn't catch him, no, but if she could get close enough for a clean shot, she'd take him out.

That was proving to be difficult. Each time she'd had an unobstructed view, he'd been waiting for her. She glanced around her, trying to determine what her options were. The drop-off on the other side of the tree was ten feet at least. High enough for her to envision a broken ankle if she landed wrong. There was a rock outcropping to her left, another ten or twelve feet away. It could give her cover, but she'd be making no progress in going down.

"Shit."

She holstered her weapon, then—before she could change her mind—she swung behind the tree, dropping the ten feet to the ledge. It was not a graceful landing as her legs gave way. She rolled to a stop at the base of a boulder the size of a small car. She waited only a few seconds before scrambling down again.

He was almost at the river now, and she could see the dark kayak tucked into the trees. His white shirt was visible through the branches, and she stood, taking aim. Before she could fire her weapon, her feet slipped from under her, and she landed on her ass as she skidded down the steep incline. He heard her and turned, shooting in her direction. He hit a rock next to her and she felt the fragments of it cut her cheek.

She was on another ledge. This was her last chance, she knew. He'd be in the river and gone in a matter of seconds. She stood up, now only forty feet from him, if that. He was untying the kayak, about to launch.

"Police!" she yelled. *Shit.* "FBI!"

When he turned toward her, she fired. But so did he. She saw him flinch at almost the exact instant that she felt the white-hot blazing pain in her left shoulder. She lost her balance and tumbled off the ledge, landing in a heap only feet from the river.

The sky was a beautiful dark blue.

Then it turned black.

CHAPTER FORTY-EIGHT

Haley was speeding up River Road, taking curves far too fast, she knew. She had no business being out there in the first place, but she simply couldn't stay at the saloon—helpless—for another second. That wasn't the only reason. Something— something that she couldn't explain—was pushing her. It was almost a compulsion, an urging that she was needed somehow.

She slowed when she saw the familiar sign for Sam's River Runners. She spotted Carter's SUV and she pulled up beside it.

"Haley? What the hell are you doing here?" Sam called from the doorway. "Get up here."

She hurried up to the porch, pausing to look to the river where Mike and two deputies were. "What's going on?"

"Mike said he expects this guy to come downriver in the kayak he stole. They're running a cable to the other side. Get inside now. There's been shooting up by the falls. Mike said that FBI agent followed the guy down the mountain."

Haley's eyes widened. "On foot? Like hiked down?"

"Yeah. Haven't heard shooting in a little while though. Maybe she got him."

She pulled her phone out, calling Carter. After five rings, it went to voice mail, and she listened to Carter's voice for a second or two before ending the call. "Has Mike heard from her?" she asked weakly.

"I don't think so."

He closed the door and led her over to the big window that looked out to the river. Mike was wet from his waist down and both deputies appeared to be too. She saw them motioning and then Mike ran upstream, his gun in his hand. She tensed, finding herself squeezing Sam's arm tightly. Then the kayak appeared, shooting fast through the water, speeding by at an alarming rate.

She could hear Mike yell but couldn't make out his words. Just as she thought the kayak would zip past them, the deputies pulled at a wire, stretching the cable tight across the river. The guy was knocked off and the kayak went flying down the river without him.

"There goes my goddamn kayak," Sam muttered.

Mike and one of the deputies splashed in the water, going after the man who appeared to be riding the current, then he went under.

Her fingers dug into Sam's arm. "He's going to drown."

"Hell, they all could."

Sam ran outside and she followed. He grabbed three life vests from a raft and ran to the river's edge, tossing them into the water toward Mike. The deputy who stayed behind was on his phone, talking quickly and pointing at the river at the same time. Her breath caught as Mike got swept away. If not for the red vest he'd grabbed, she imagined the current would have sucked him under.

Then it was all over with as quickly as it had started. Mike was in the shallows on the other side, roughly cuffing the man, then dragging him upstream to where the cable was. From where she was, she could tell the man was injured. Blood poured from his right side, and he fell to his knees several times. Mike didn't seem to care as he jerked him up each time.

"You think it's all over with?" she asked Sam.

"I hope to hell it is."

She took out her phone again, calling Carter once more. Like before, it went unanswered.

"Lock this son of a bitch up," Mike said as he handed the guy over to the deputies.

Haley could see that he was bleeding profusely and barely seemed to be conscious. No one seemed to be concerned with it as they shoved him roughly into the back of their car. Mike looked startled to find her there.

"Haley?" Then he grinned. "This was kind of a letdown, wasn't it? I wanted to shoot the bastard. Hell, he must have lost his gun in the river. Didn't even have a weapon on him."

"Where's Carter?"

"Hopefully up at the falls. She got this guy pretty good. With luck, he'll die on the way back down the mountain," he said crudely.

"I called her. She didn't answer." She walked closer to him. "I got a bad feeling."

He nodded. "Yeah. Okay. We'll drive as close as we can and hike in." He touched her arm. "I think she's probably okay. Maybe her phone drowned in the river or something."

"Yeah. Maybe so."

She wished she could have his optimism, but she didn't.

CHAPTER FORTY-NINE

As Haley practically ran through the trees, she could hear the roar of the falls and little else. She hadn't visited the falls in a very long time. There was a hiking trail farther up that would take you to the base of the falls. When she first moved there, she'd gone often to sit and watch.

To sit and watch and think of Gail. Think of Gail and hope to get a sign or to feel her presence or something. She never did and she eventually stopped going. Instead, she would take long, exhausting hikes that seemed to clear her mind and ease her heartache, at least for a little while.

It was Carter now, not Gail. Carter who she was rushing to find with Mike right behind her. Finally she could see the river. She pushed on faster, ducking through the branches of a young spruce tree. At the water's edge, she paused to catch her breath. Mike bent over at the waist, gasping.

"Damn, I ain't as young as I used to be."

"You kept up pretty good for an old man." She turned toward the falls, feeling the spray on her face as the wind carried it. Then she looked up at the mountain on the other side. "How far was she?"

"I don't think this close to the falls."

They walked downstream, and she kept her gaze glued to the opposite shoreline. She wished Carter had worn something bright, something that would stand out, but she knew she'd been in her usual black FBI T-shirt. She stopped, seeing nothing out of the ordinary.

"Carter!" she called loudly. "Carter?" She knew that was most likely futile. The sound of the falls would have drowned her out.

"Is that her?" Mike pointed downstream. "I didn't bring my damn binoculars."

Haley shielded her eyes against the sun, her heart lodging in her throat. "Yes," she breathed and took off running.

Carter was on her back, arms and legs lifeless. "Oh god," she murmured as she grabbed Mike's arm. "Can we get across with the rope?"

He dropped the rope he'd thought to bring along and walked slowly downstream a bit farther. "It's deep here. Let's go down a little ways. Rope or not, we'd get sucked into one of these holes." He picked the rope up again. "Come on."

They hurried downstream, and she glanced back several times at Carter, who hadn't moved. Her chest hurt at the sight.

"Do you think she's…" *What?* Dead? Alive?

"Won't do no good to think the worst."

No, but that didn't stop the awful churning of her stomach. It was a feeling she knew well. She pushed it aside now, ignoring the pain she felt. It was there, under the surface, waiting for her, though. She knew it wouldn't be far away. It never was.

They had gone downstream at least fifty yards, maybe more when Mike stopped. "Here. See the rocks in the middle. I think I can make it across. Tie the rope to me, you anchor it here."

She shook her head. "No. I won't be able to hold you. Let me go across. If I slip and go down, I know you're strong enough to stop me."

"It should be me. I—"

"Let's don't argue." She tugged at the rope he had, hoping it was long enough to reach the other side. He took it from her, tying it at her waist.

"Why the hell didn't we grab life vests? Shit, I had one on. I took it off."

"I'll be fine." She took a tentative step into the river, then turned back to him. "You won't let me go, right?"

He gave her a quick grin. "You're my best friend. Of course I won't let you go."

She nodded quickly, then walked fully into the cold water, holding her hands out to her sides to help balance. As she got farther away from shore—five feet, six feet—she felt the river tugging at her legs. She was up to her waist now, barely able to fight the current that threatened to sweep her downstream.

She kept going, inching along, her feet becoming numb from the icy torrent. As she got deeper, her footing was precarious at best. In a flash, the current took her, whipping her down like a sodden fallen log. She came up spitting out water. She rolled to her back—as she'd learned to do—not fighting the water. She felt the tautness of the rope, and she raised her hand out of the water, giving Mike a thumbs-up.

When she felt the rocks again, she righted herself, turning sideways as she walked. She was getting closer now, past the deep cut in the center and into shallower water. It was at her waist again and a few feet farther, to her thighs.

"That's it," Mike called. "No more rope."

"Okay. I think I can make it from here."

She untied the knot he'd made at her waist, not caring that as soon as she dropped it, it would shoot downstream with the current. She tossed it aside, then carefully made her way into the rocky, shallow shoreline. Once on dry land, she ran upstream, her wet jeans and soggy boots making her feel heavy and laden. She felt like she was running in slow motion toward Carter.

As she got closer, she saw blood on Carter's face, her arm. She braced herself for what she might find, wishing that she'd let Mike cross the river instead. She wasn't strong enough for this—she wasn't prepared. Nonetheless, she ran on, finally falling to her knees beside Carter.

"Oh my god," she murmured. Her hand was shaking as she reached out and touched Carter's face. "Carter? Are you… god…Carter?"

Her skin felt cool, damp. Or maybe it was the cold she was feeling from being in the river. She let her fingers slide to Carter's neck and nearly sobbed with relief as she felt a pulse.

"She's alive!" she called to Mike. "Get help!"

Then she leaned closer to Carter, touching her face again. "Carter? Can you hear me? Can you open your eyes, sweetie?"

She watched as Carter's eyelids fluttered but didn't open.

"Am I dead?" came a hoarse whisper. "I hear angels."

"Oh, honey. How bad is it?"

"I don't know. Not so bad, I guess. Everything is kinda numb." Her eyes opened a tiny bit, then she closed them again. "I saw the kid."

Haley frowned. "The kid?"

"The kid with the toy gun. He was here. He was in the sky. He was smiling at me, like he was forgiving me for killing him. So when I saw the kid, I thought for sure I was going to die. Or maybe I was already dead. Am I?" Her speech was slow, slurred and Haley grabbed her hand, squeezing it tightly.

"Carter, please stay with me. Please?" She leaned closer. "I can't lose you too. I don't think I could take that."

Carter's hand felt limp in her own and she nearly panicked. Again, she touched her neck, still feeling her pulse. She turned to the opposite side of the river where Mike stood watching.

"She spoke to me," she called. "I think she's unconscious now."

"Chopper is on the way. Ten minutes," he yelled back to her.

Ten minutes would be an eternity.

CHAPTER FIFTY

As soon as the helicopter flew away—taking Carter with it—Haley turned to Mike, nearly falling into his arms.

"She's going to be okay," he said as he held her. "They...they think she's going to be okay."

Haley nodded against his shoulder, then pulled away, embarrassed that there were tears in her eyes. She wiped them away impatiently.

"Yes, I know. I think she'll be fine. But then..."

"Then?"

She gave a sad smile. "Then she'll leave me."

"So you let her in, huh?"

"I did. She's been here what? Eight, ten days? I feel like I've known her for years. It was just so easy."

"Yeah, me too. But let's don't run her out of town just yet. Let's go get cleaned up, then we'll head down the mountain. Maybe we'll splurge. Go out to eat somewhere."

She linked arms with him as they headed back to Carter's SUV. "Mexican food and a margarita."

"Sounds good to me."

* * *

The hospital waiting room was brightly lit and nearly empty, which she assumed was a good thing. There was a TV on, but the sound was muted. An older couple with who appeared to be their grandchild was sitting at the far end. A family of four sat talking quietly on the next row. She and Mike were sitting by themselves, neither talking. All they knew was that Carter was still in surgery.

The news had spread around town that the killer had been captured. According to Mike, the campgrounds would be opening up again as soon as tomorrow, and both the lodge and motel were calling guests, trying to get them back. "It'll all get back to normal soon," he'd said.

Yes. Normal. Back to business. What did that mean though? What *was* normal? She didn't know anymore. Her life felt like it had been turned upside down in a matter of weeks. The familiar, comforting pain in her heart was gone, replaced with a completely new kind of ache. She'd been so lonely after Gail had died, after she'd been left behind. Her future seemed so bleak, she hadn't wanted to even contemplate it. So yes, she knew loneliness. That was *her* normal.

Why then did the prospect of Carter leaving bring such sadness to her? Why did she fear this loneliness that she was about to endure? As the saying goes, been there, done that. Maybe she was dreading it because she'd had a reprieve and she now knew what her life could be like with someone in it, someone other than Gail. And really, except for Mike, Carter was her only friend. She would miss that, certainly. And she would miss the closeness they'd established—the intimacy. As she'd told Mike, it was so easy with Carter. Effortless, really. Both their friendship and the sex.

Maybe what she really feared was that when Carter left Timber Falls, she would sink into that dark place again, that place that was heavy and thick...and dead.

Mike nudged her arm, bringing her out of her musings.

"You're twisting that ring on your finger like you're spinning a top."

She glanced down, not even aware she'd been doing that. She held her hand up, staring at the wedding band Gail had given her. Its twin was buried with Gail.

"You think I should take it off?"

He shrugged. "I guess it depends on the reason you wear it in the first place. Do you still feel married? Or is it a reminder that you *were* married?"

"I don't need a reminder. At first, yes, I still felt married. The thought of taking it off never occurred to me, really." She touched the band again. "I think taking it off would have meant that I was letting her go."

Mike covered her hand, hiding the ring from her gaze. "Then yes, I think you should take it off."

CHAPTER FIFTY-ONE

"Who is here for Agent Carter?"

Mike stood quickly. "We are. I'm Chief Goodson, Timber Falls Police Department."

The doctor nodded and Haley could see how weary he looked. "Agent Carter made it through surgery fine. The entry wound was here," he said, touching his upper left chest. "The trajectory of the bullet indicates that she was shot from below. It missed her heart by centimeters, fortunately. It traveled up," he said, again touching himself, "and lodged in her shoulder. She's very lucky. We did some reconstruction, but she should recover fully."

"That's great news," Mike said. "Thank you."

"May we see her?" Haley asked.

"She's still sedated, but you can sit with her for a few moments, if you like. I'll have a nurse take you to her room."

They followed him back, then a nurse led them down a long corridor. "You may stay for ten minutes," she said as she pushed open a door.

The darkness of the room was a stark contrast to the brightness of the corridor. Blinds were pulled tight across the window and only a dim lamp was on. Haley stared at the IV drip, the needle stuck into the top of Carter's hand. The monitor on the wall gave a steady, comforting beep.

"She looks pale," Haley whispered.

"Yeah, she does."

She moved closer, taking Carter's hand gently. It was soft and warm, and she closed her eyes, so thankful that Carter was okay. So thankful that she was alive.

"You want a few minutes alone?"

She looked back at Mike, knowing she had tears in her eyes. "Do you mind?"

"No. I'll wait in the hallway."

The door clicked shut behind him and she turned back to Carter, letting her tears fall. "I was…I was really scared, Carter. When you were lying there, when I saw the blood, I thought… well, I thought you were dead. And I didn't know how that made me feel." She wiped at her tears and tried to blink them away. "You've become…well, special to me. You chased away my loneliness and made me feel like a woman again." She kissed Carter's hand, resting her cheek on it. "I don't want you to leave, Carter. I'm going to miss you being around, you know." She lifted her head. "So I don't want you to leave me." She wiped her tears again. "No. I don't want you to leave. But I know you will." She tried to smile. "I just don't want to think about it yet."

She stood up then, feeling foolish. "I'm sorry. I'm a mess." She spotted a box of tissues and pulled a couple out, blowing her nose. "So I guess I'm going to leave. The nurse said ten minutes."

She took a step away, then went back, bending over to kiss Carter on the lips. "I'm so glad you're okay," she whispered. "And I can't wait to see you again."

The door opened and she turned, finding the nurse there. She nodded at her, then looked back at Carter one last time.

"Will you tell her that Haley and Mike were here, please."

"Of course."

She paused on the way out. "Do you know how long she'll be in?"

"It depends. If there are no setbacks, probably only two days."

"Oh, that's great. Thank you."

Mike gave her a quick hug. "You okay?"

"I don't know, honestly." She smiled at him. "I could use a margarita."

"Yeah. Let's go."

CHAPTER FIFTY-TWO

Carter pulled to a stop in front of the saloon, surprised by the number of cars in town. Apparently it hadn't taken long for the river rats to return. And why not? It was a gorgeous summer day with endless blue skies. She got out of her SUV, careful of her injured shoulder. She supposed she'd get used to the sling soon enough, considering she'd be using it for six weeks.

She turned around, looking up River Road, hearing laughter as a raft came shooting down. She watched it until it passed, then turned her gaze back down Main Street, a smile on her face as she looked at the now familiar sight. Damn, but she was thankful to get to see this again.

Mike and Haley had come to see her both days, dropping her rented SUV off on the second day. They'd had a nice, long visit, and she appreciated them taking the time out of their days to do that. She especially appreciated that Haley had brought her a burger and steak fries. They hadn't had a second alone, though. Mike told her he'd had the chance to speak to Edward Dickenson. He was in the same hospital as she was. His injury was a little more serious than hers. They'd had to remove part of his liver. He told them where they could find the bodies of his wife and the prosecutor, Eric Crumpton. He'd dumped them out in the desert south of Vegas.

"I asked him why he didn't cut my throat when he had the chance. He said he wanted me to suffer the same fate that he had." Mike had shaken his head. "It's messed up, man. He went into prison a sane person, but he didn't come out that way."

No. Obviously not. But it was over now. Life in this little mountain village would get back to normal.

She looked up into the sky, the bright blueness of it nearly hurting her eyes. She looked around up there, searching for a face, a shape. She'd seen the kid. She was certain of that. Or maybe not. It would be crazy if she had. Maybe her subconscious had called him up, though she wanted to believe that he'd been there, that he'd forgiven her. She supposed she'd never know for sure.

With one last look around, she headed to the saloon. She couldn't wait to see Haley. But the ringing of her phone made her pause. It was Murdock. He'd been calling her three or four times a day. With a sigh, she pulled it from her pocket.

"Hey, Carter here."

"Agent Carter, I understand you've been released."

"Yeah. Thought I told you today was the day."

"And I thought I told you to stay an extra day."

She smiled. "They don't actually give you a choice, Murdock. They basically kicked me out."

"What about rehab?"

"Yeah, something to look forward to. Gotta say, your insurance is top-notch. The physical therapist is going to come up here three days a week."

"Up here where?"

She looked through the window of the saloon, seeing Haley moving about inside. "Timber Falls. Gonna hang out here for a while."

"Why there? It's going to be six weeks. Thought you'd head back to LA for your rehab."

"Got nothing there. Made a couple of friends here." She looked up River Road again. "I've kinda fallen in love with this little town."

There was an unnatural pause before he spoke. "You *are* planning on coming back to work, right? I'll have the motorhome ready to go."

She paused too. "To be honest, I don't know. I feel like I'm at a crossroads, maybe." She looked at the saloon, seeing the HELP WANTED sign in the window. She smiled. "I may want to hang around here."

"And do what, Carter?"

"I don't know. Just live, I guess."

"Look, don't make any hasty decisions, Carter. You had a traumatic experience. Take some time. Do your rehab. In six weeks, you'll probably be ready to move on."

She nodded. "Yeah. I'll do that." She looked up into the blue sky again. "I feel damn lucky to be alive, you know. I just want to embrace that."

"I understand. Take your time. You did a damn good job with this case, Carter. Jason told me he wasn't much help to you."

"Oh, I don't know. Jason figured out who the guy was. It all worked out."

"Yeah, it did."

"Yeah, so I've got a beer calling my name."

"A beer? Should you be drinking?"

"Probably not. One won't kill me. I'll talk to you later, Murdock."

"Okay. I'll check in on you."

The line went dead, and she felt free for some reason. Sure, she knew he'd call and probably pressure her to make a decision, but she knew she didn't have to. Not right now. She walked up the steps to the saloon, then went inside. The familiar jingle of the bell made her smile. Instead of going to the bar, she went to the window and plucked out the HELP WANTED sign.

Haley was at the bar, watching her. Carter gave her a grin. "Hey."

"Hey yourself."

Carter held the sign up. "You hiring?"

Haley met her gaze. "I am."

Carter nodded. "I can start on Monday."

Haley smiled at her. "It doesn't pay much."

"Okay. To compensate, I'll need free food and beer."

"I'm agreeable to that." Then she laughed. "Are you serious?"

"Well, I've got six weeks off. Rehab. I thought I could do it up here. If Mike will let me stay at his place, that is."

Haley shook her head. "No. You can stay with me."

"Are you sure?"

"Very."

She pointed at her sling. "I'm supposed to sleep in this thing, so…"

Haley laughed again. "We'll work around it. You want a beer?"

"I do. Just one. I'm still on meds." She glanced around. "Got more people in town already, huh?"

"Yeah. Word has spread, apparently. Scott said that the lodge is booked again, and the campgrounds opened up yesterday. By the weekend, I'm sure the town will be packed."

The bell jingled and she turned, seeing Bill and Charlie coming inside. They both nodded a greeting at her.

"You're back," Charlie said. "No worse for wear?"

"Just a wounded wing. Not too bad."

"Let me buy you a beer," Bill said. "It was good to have you here."

"Thanks. I'm going to stick around for a little while." She looked at Haley. "See what happens."

CHAPTER FIFTY-THREE

Haley found herself smiling—and holding her breath—as Carter held her arms out to her sides, balancing on the fallen log as she crossed over the small creek. The six weeks had come and gone but not without dread as each day ticked by. They fit so perfectly together, there had been no awkwardness with Carter sharing her home and her bed. But she'd been counting down the weeks, nonetheless. Then one morning as Carter had been juggling four breakfast orders at once, she casually mentioned that she might "hang around a bit longer" if that was okay with her. Not another word had been spoken about her leaving. That was a month ago.

And here they were, taking a Sunday break, hiking to Timber Falls. Haley didn't kid herself. She knew she was falling in love with Carter. Oh, hell, she was probably already in love with her. That scared her, of course. Would Carter leave eventually? Or was Carter in love too? She'd not said the words, no, but when they made love, the way Carter looked at her, she would swear that she was. And again, that scared her too.

"You coming or what?"

Haley nodded. "I want to get a dog. A puppy."

"Oh yeah?"

"Yeah. What do you think?"

"I think that would be great. But what about when we're both working? Then what will we do with her?"

"Her?"

"Or him. I think we might be violating some health code if we brought him to work."

"I could stash him in the office. Or her."

"You know what we could do. We could put a fence around the back, and he could stay out there."

"Behind the saloon?"

"Yeah. Out the kitchen door."

She held her arms out, mimicking Carter as she walked across the log to the other side. Carter took her hand and pulled her close, kissing her on the mouth.

"It's been a great day."

"Yes, it has." She took Carter's hand. "Are you going to leave me?"

Carter stopped walking. "Do we need to talk?"

"Yes, I think it's time."

Carter nodded. "Okay."

She continued down the trail to the falls and Haley followed. The sound of water crashing onto rocks was getting louder and she could make out the river through the trees now. She took a deep breath, then blurted out the words she'd wanted to say for a while now.

"I'm falling in love with you."

Carter stopped and turned around. A smile was on her face. "Oh yeah?"

"Uh-huh."

"That's good."

"Is it? Are you planning on leaving me?"

Carter came toward her then. "When my six weeks was up, I told Murdock I didn't want to leave here. He's kinda holding my job for me still, in case I change my mind."

"And will you?"

Carter's eyes softened. "I'm crazy about you, Haley. But I know Gail has a place in your heart and I didn't know if there was room for me there too."

Haley swallowed. "Are you in love with me?"

Carter nodded. "I think that's what this is."

Haley went closer, going into her arms. Their hug was tight, and their kiss was hard and long. When she pulled away, she saw love reflected back at her in Carter's eyes. She nodded but said nothing else. They held hands as they walked to the river.

The falls weren't quite as fierce as they were in early summer. The river was losing its power as summer shifted to fall. But it was still beautiful and mighty and she and Carter both stared at it.

"Does it bother you to come here?" she asked.

Carter shook her head. "Not at all, no." She pointed to the opposite side, up the mountain a ways. "That's where I fell from. It doesn't look that high now, but at the time…"

"Yes, I imagine so."

Carter turned to her. "I'm sorry. I guess Gail—"

"Completely different. She was chasing another mountain peak. You were chasing a killer." She turned to her. "There's room in my heart for you, Carter. A lot of room. It's been so long, I don't feel her anymore. It's just memories, but I don't have that ache any longer. You've filled me with light and chased all that darkness away."

She took Carter's hand and tugged her closer to the falls. "I want to say goodbye to her. It's time."

Carter looked at her quizzically, and Haley held up her hand, slipping the wedding band from her finger.

"I don't need this anymore."

"You don't want to keep it?"

"No. I loved her, I did. But she's gone." She looked at Carter. "I never once thought I would find love again. I never thought I'd even try. But you walked into my life, and everything changed. In the blink of an eye, everything changed, Carter." She held the ring up. "I don't want to live in the past. I'm in love with you and it feels so good to say that."

She fingered the ring for a second longer, then tossed it into the falls. The freedom she felt was profound, and she tilted her head back and laughed. Carter turned her around and pulled her into an embrace. Yes, she truly was free.

"I'd forgotten what it felt like to be in love. It's rather nice."

Carter grinned. "It's a first for me. But I kinda like it too."

Bella Books, Inc.

Women. Books. Even Better Together.

P.O. Box 10543
Tallahassee, FL 32302

Phone: 800-729-4992
www.bellabooks.com